"I'm sorry," he said. "I don't know who you are."

She sighed. "I hoped you would—that you might..."

"Why?" he asked.

"Because it would've made this easier if you were expecting me," she replied.

Expecting her? He hadn't been expecting anything else—not the bombs or the shootings being meant for him. Why the hell would he have expected her?

"Make what easier?" he asked.

Was she a hit woman? A hired assassin?

He glanced around for his holster and weapon—but it, like his clothes, were nowhere in sight. Neither was any of his damn family.

He'd thought they weren't going to leave him alone....

"What I have to tell you," she said. Then she drew in a deep breath, as if to brace herself, and continued, "That this is your son."

BRIDEGROOM BODYGUARD

LISA CHILDS

Recycling programs for this product may not exist in your area.

With much love and appreciation for my daughters Ashley & Chloe Theeuwes. You are both exceptionally smart and strong and beautiful young women. You have made your mother very proud!

ISBN-13: 978-0-373-69778-6

BRIDEGROOM BODYGUARD

This edition published by arrangement with Harlequin Books S.A.

For questions and comments about the quality of this book, please contact us at CustomerService@Harlequin.com.

Printed in U.S.A.

ABOUT THE AUTHOR

Bestselling, award-winning author Lisa Childs writes paranormal and contemporary romance for Harlequin. She lives on thirty acres in Michigan with her two daughters, a talkative Siamese and a long-haired Chihuahua who thinks she's a rottweiler. Lisa loves hearing from readers, who can contact her through her website, www.lisachilds.com, or snail-mail address, P.O. Box 139, Marne, MI 49435.

Books by Lisa Childs

HARLEQUIN INTRIGUE

664—RETURN OF THE LAWMAN
720—SARAH'S SECRETS
758—BRIDAL RECONNAISSANCE
834—THE SUBSTITUTE SISTER
1213—MYSTERY LOVER
1263—RANSOM FOR A PRINCE
1318—DADDY BOMBSHELL
1338—LAWMAN LOVER*
1344—BABY BREAKOUT*
1403—PROTECTING THE PREGNANT PRINCESS§
1410—THE PRINCESS PREDICAMENT§
1417—ROYAL RESCUE§
1500—GROOM UNDER FIRE‡
1506—EXPLOSIVE ENGAGEMENT‡
1511—BRIDEGROOM BODYGUARD‡

*Outlaws
§Royal Bodyguards
‡Shotgun Weddings

CAST OF CHARACTERS

Parker Payne—The bodyguard has a bounty on his head and a baby he didn't know about, but his biggest problem is Sharon Wells and the protective and passionate feelings she brings out in this bachelor.

Sharon Wells—She has no idea how she became the target of hired assassins or the bride of a confirmed bachelor, and she's afraid that she won't survive the honeymoon.

Logan Payne—Parker's twin keeps being mistaken for Parker, and it may cost him his life.

Judge Brenda Foster—Sharon's employer may be the one who put her life at risk.

Chuck Horowitz—The judge's new bodyguard doesn't have the integrity of Payne Protection Agency.

Detective Sharpe—The lawman thinks Parker and Sharon know more than they do about who wants them dead.

Garek & Milek Kozminski—Logan's new brothers-in-law might have found a way to protect their sister from the dangers of being part of the Payne family—by carrying out the hit and collecting the reward.

Cooper Payne—The former marine cut his honeymoon short to protect his brother, but his resemblance to Parker puts him in danger, too.

Nikki Payne—The female bodyguard is sick of her big brothers trying to protect her when they're the ones who actually need protecting.

FBI agent Nicholas Rus—The agent has been brought in to investigate the River City Police Department, but he seems more interested in the Payne family.

Penny Payne—The matchmaking Payne matriarch only wants what's best for her children, even though she didn't have the ideal marriage herself.

Judge Munson—He's helped out Penny Payne in the past, but he might have ulterior motives.

Chapter One

Someone put out a hit on Parker Payne.

The statement echoed inside Parker's head, but it wasn't the only echo. His ears rang yet from the blast of the explosion that had sent him to the hospital and two Payne Protection Agency employees to the morgue.

Guilt and pain clutched his heart. He was supposed to have been inside that SUV, not Douglas and Terry. But, totally unaware of the bomb that had been wired to the ignition, they had jumped inside his vehicle for a lunch run. He'd been rushing out to catch them to change an order, but he had been too late. Doug turned the key, and the SUV exploded into bits of glass and scraps of metal. Two good men died, leaving behind wives and children.

It should have been Parker. Not only did he have no wife or child to leave behind, but he was actually the one whom somebody wanted dead.

He fought against the pain and confusion of the concussion that had his head pounding and his vision blurred. So he closed his eyes and tried to focus on the conversation swirling around his hospital bed.

His mother fussed. "We should take this conversation into the hall so that Parker can get some rest." Her fingers skimmed across his forehead, like they had when he'd been a little boy with a fever or a scraped knee or when his father died. She had always been there for her kids even though she hadn't had anyone to be there for her.

He caught her hand and gently squeezed her fingers in reassurance. She had to be scared at how close she had come to losing a child. In the past two weeks, there had been several attempts on his brother Cooper's life and on his twin Logan's life. But most of those attempts had really been meant to end *his* life.

Logan bossed. "We need to find out who the hell put out the hit." Then his tone turned suspicious, so he must have been addressing one of his new in-laws, when he added, "Unless you already know. Your *contacts* must have told you who when they told you about the hit."

The guy cursed Logan, so he must have been the hot-headed Garek instead of the milder-mannered Milek Kozminski. "If I knew who the hell it is, I would have told you—the monster put my sister in danger."

Parker forced open his eyes, but he had to squint against the glare of the overhead lights and the sunlight streaming through the blinds. His head pounded harder, but it was more with guilt than pain. Stacy Kozminski-Payne had been through a lot recently, most of it because of him. He focused on his new sister-in-law. The tawny-haired woman stood between her husband and her brother, as if ready to stop a brawl. It was probably a position in which she would find herself for most of her marriage.

But then his twin did something Logan rarely did; he apologized. "Sorry, man. I know you would do anything to protect your sister."

Garek nodded in acceptance of the apology and continued, "The only thing I know for certain is that it's somebody who has a lot of money and influence."

"You and Milek need to reach out to all your contacts and see what you can find out." Logan resumed his bossing. As CEO of Payne Protection Agency and the oldest Payne sibling by ten minutes, he'd gotten good at giving out orders.

But the Kozminskis weren't known for taking orders well, so Parker waited for them to bristle. Instead Milek asked, "Are you really hiring us?"

Payne Protection Agency was a security firm that Logan had founded when he'd left the police department a few years ago. He'd coerced Parker into leaving the force, too, and joining him. Logan had always been very selective about who he hired—that was why Terry and Douglas had been such good men and their deaths such a tragic loss.

Through narrowed blue eyes, Logan studied his new brothers-in-law. Very new since he and Stacy had married only hours ago in Parker's hospital room so that he could be Logan's best man. "I need your help," he said. And Parker knew his twin so well that he knew that wasn't an easy admission for him to make.

Stacy knew her husband well, too, because she hugged him in appreciation and sympathy. And love. It was obvious how much she loved him. And Logan loved her just as much.

So much that Parker felt a pang of envy. God, he must have hit his head harder than he'd realized.

His arms winding around his wife, Logan continued, "We need to keep Stacy and Parker safe."

And finally Parker managed to fight back the pain and gather his strength. He struggled to swing his legs over the bed and sit up. "This isn't your fight, Logan," he said. "It's mine. So you're not giving out the orders this time."

He had never minded before that Logan was his boss as well as his brother, but he minded now—because he didn't want his boss or his brother getting killed. "I'm not hiring Payne Protection. I can take care of this myself." Now that he knew he was the intended target...

Logan turned to him as if surprised to find him still in the room. "Parker—"

"This is all about me," he said. "And you need to be all about your new bride. You and Stacy need to leave for your honeymoon."

Logan's arms tightened protectively around his bride, but he shook his head. "I'm not leaving while you're in danger."

"That's exactly why you have to leave," Parker pointed out. "Because when I'm in danger, so are you." With the same black hair and blue eyes and chiseled features, they were so identical that most people couldn't tell them apart unless they knew them. Logan was always serious, and Parker was usually a smart aleck.

Logan shook his head. "That's exactly why we need to all work together to find out who put out the hit on you."

"Probably a jealous husband," a male voice remarked as another man stepped into the hospital room.

"Cooper!" their mother exclaimed over her youngest son.

Even though he was two years younger than Parker and Logan, he could have been their triplet. He looked that much like them. "Damn it," Parker grumbled. "You should still be on your honeymoon."

And that was when it struck him that both his brothers were husbands now. Only he and his baby sister were single yet. And his mom. But she was widowed, so that was different.

He didn't want his new sisters-in-law to become widows, too. "You need to take Tanya and get on a plane and get the hell out of here. And take Logan and Stacy with you."

"Logan and Stacy?" Cooper stared at the woman wrapped up in his oldest brother's arms, and his dark brows arched in shock. Logan and Stacy had spent the past several years hating each other before finally but quickly realizing that they actually loved each other. And they hadn't come to that realization until Cooper and Tanya had left for their honeymoon.

"Parker is getting upset," his mother said. "And he needs his rest. Maybe having Logan and Stacy's wedding in his room was too much for him—"

"Wedding!" Cooper interjected.

Their mother shushed him. "You all need to take the explanations and orders into the hall." Her tone had grown sharper and her usually warm brown eyes were dark with concern and determination.

Her children and even the Kozminskis hurried to obey her, nearly bumping into each other in their haste to step out into the hall. She gently pushed Parker back against the pillows. "The doctor is keeping you overnight for observation," she reminded him, which was probably good since the concussion had affected his short-term memory. "So you really need to rest."

"Mom—"

"You'll need all of your strength to fight with your brothers," she said, dredging up the argument she had used when he'd been a kid reluctant to go to bed. She kissed his forehead before joining the rest of their dysfunctional family in the hall.

Finally Parker was alone. He was also exhausted. But when he closed his eyes, the explosion played out behind his lids. He saw the men through the windshield—just briefly—before the glass shattered and the metal shredded and their bodies…

With a groan of horror and pain, he jerked awake and discovered that he was no longer alone. A woman stood over his bed. She wasn't a nurse—at least not one employed at the hospital—because she didn't wear the green scrubs. She wore a suit with tan pants and a high-necked blouse beneath a loose tan jacket. So he might have thought she worked in hospital administration if not for the baby she balanced on one lean hip.

"You're Parker Payne," she said.

He tensed with suspicion. Why did she want to know? Then he pushed aside the suspicions. It wasn't as if she was trying to collect on that hit—unless hired assassins brought their babies along with them, too.

And if they did, he would rather she try to hit *him* than Logan or Cooper. "Yes, I'm Parker Payne."

She released a shuddery breath of relief. "You're not dead."

"Not yet." But it wasn't for want of people trying.

She shuddered. "I saw on the news what happened to you—or nearly happened to you. It was your vehicle…"

"I'm fine," he said with a twinge of guilt at the unfairness of that. Doug and Terry should be fine, too, but they were gone, leaving family behind just like Parker had been left when his police-officer father died in the line of duty.

At least if someone was actually successful at carrying out the hit, he wouldn't leave a child behind to mourn him like he had mourned. His family and friends thought he stayed single because he couldn't commit, because he was a playboy. But he was practical. Given the dangerous nature of his job, he wasn't a good risk for a husband or father. And he didn't want to put anyone through the pain he, his mother and siblings had suffered.

The woman studied him through narrowed eyes. Even narrowed, her eerie light brown eyes were so huge that they nearly overwhelmed her thin face. If her hair was down, the caramel-colored locks might have softened her face, but it was pulled tautly back and bound in a tight knot on the top of her head. Her voice low and soft, she asked, "Are you sure you're all right?"

He shook off his maudlin thoughts. He wasn't going to leave anyone behind because he wasn't going to die—at least not before he found out who was after him and made that person pay for all the pain he'd caused. Parker had rested long enough, so he swung his legs over the bed again and sat up. His vision blurred for a moment, but he blinked to clear it.

"Should I get someone?" she asked as she backed up toward the door. She jostled the baby on her hip, and the little thing giggled.

Parker focused on the baby. Dressed in tiny overalls and a blue-and-green-striped shirt, he was apparently a boy. With fuzzy black hair and bright blue eyes, he was also damn cute.

"You know who I am," he realized. "But I don't know who you are. Should I?" He usually never forgot a face—at least not a female one. But she wore no makeup and dressed so frumpy that she wasn't exactly the kind of woman he usually noticed…unless he was in the mood for the repressed-librarian type. And maybe he was in the mood now because he was tempted to see what she would look like with her hair down…

"My name is Sharon Wells," she told him, her soft voice questioning as if she wondered if he remembered it.

As if he should…

He moved his head to shake it, but even the slight movement sent pain radiating throughout his skull. He groaned.

"I should get someone," she said again with a nervous glance toward the hall. "You need help."

"No." He already had too many people trying to help him, trying to fix a problem he must have somehow created himself. The hit was on *him*—no one else. Who had he pissed off enough to want him dead?

Cooper was wrong about the jealous husband. Parker had never messed around with a married woman and never would; there were lines even he refused to cross.

"I don't need anyone," he said.

Now she glanced down at the baby she bounced gently on her hip. His arms flailed, and his chubby little face flushed with happiness. Even though they looked nothing alike, it was as if the child was a part of her because they were so connected.

"Sharon Wells…" He repeated her name but it didn't sound familiar even on his own lips. She wasn't Doug's or Terry's wife; he knew their names, their faces, which he would never be able to look at again without a rush of guilt and shame. If Sharon Wells was a relative of one of them, she must've been a distant one, because he'd met most of their families, too.

He pushed up from the bed and stood on legs that were embarrassingly shaky until he locked his knees.

He wasn't staying overnight in the hospital, not when he had a killer to track down. "I'm sorry," he said. "I don't know who you are."

She sighed. "I hoped you would, that you might…"

"Why?" he asked.

"Because it would've made this easier if you were expecting me," she replied.

Expecting her? He hadn't been expecting anything else—not the bombs or the shootings to be meant for him. Why would he have expected her?

"Make what easier?" he asked.

Was she a hit woman? A hired assassin?

He glanced around for his holster and weapon, but they, like his clothes, were nowhere in sight. Neither was any of his family.

He'd thought they weren't going to leave him alone…

"What I have to tell you," she said. Then she drew in a deep breath, as if to brace herself, and continued, "That this is your son."

He focused on the baby again. The little guy had fuzzy black hair and very bright blue eyes. The kid looked exactly like old baby pictures of him and Logan and Cooper. The baby certainly could have been a Payne. He could have been Parker's…

Maybe he did need longer to recover from the concussion because standing was so much of a strain that his head grew light, and his knees gave out. His already banged-up body struck the floor. Hard. The last thing he heard, before oblivion claimed him, was her scream.

Chapter Two

She shouldn't have screamed, but his falling was such a shock that it slipped out. And started a commotion. Ethan screamed, too—his was high-pitched and blood-curdling as he reacted to her fear. And people rushed into the room.

These were the people she had passed in the hall, the people posted like guards outside his room. But given the police reports she had seen about the explosion and the previous attempts on his brothers' lives, she understood the need for security. Yet they had all let her just walk past them. They had asked her no questions; they had only stared…at Ethan, their eyes round with shock.

They had immediately known what it had taken Parker much longer to realize—that she carried his son.

"What did you do to him?" one of his brothers angrily asked her as he crouched next to Parker on the floor. He looked so much like him that he could have been a twin. There were two men that good-looking in the world? It wasn't fair.

Then a third one rushed forward to help lift Parker back onto the bed. Were they actually triplets? This man's black hair was shorter—in a military brush cut, but other than that he looked so much like the other two it was uncanny. And Ethan looked like a miniature version of all of them. He must have been the spitting image of what they had looked like as babies.

Parker shrugged off his brothers' helping hands and stood up again, steadily, as if his strength had already returned. And given the way his heavily muscled arms stretched the sleeves of his hospital gown, he was strong.

"I'm all right," he assured his concerned family. "I just tried to get up too fast."

An older woman tore her concerned gaze from Parker to stare at the baby. "Or was it the shock?" Her hand trembled slightly as she reached out for one of Ethan's flailing chubby fists. When she touched him, he calmed down, his howls trailing away to soft hiccups. "Of finding out you're a daddy?"

Parker shook his head then flinched at the motion. *"Mom,"* he exclaimed with shock and exasperation. "I am *not* a daddy." He glanced at one of his brothers. "Is he yours?"

Of the group of people who'd rushed back into the room, a tawny-haired woman laughed while a blond-haired man snorted derisively.

Parker's brother's eyes widened in horror, and he glanced from Ethan to her. "I've never seen her before."

"Neither have I."

Sharon flinched. They had met a few times, albeit a while ago. How did he not remember her at all?

"You took one heck of a hit on the head," his brother reminded him. "The doctor said you might have some memory loss because of the concussion."

"Short-term memory loss," Parker clarified. "That means I might forget what happened minutes or hours ago, not months ago."

Sharon should have realized that a man like him wouldn't remember a woman like her. She had spent her life trying to be quiet and unobtrusive, so there was no wonder that so few people ever noticed her.

But then the older woman glanced up at Sharon, her brown eyes full of warmth and wonder. Her hair was auburn, with no traces of gray, so she didn't look old enough to have three thirtysomething-old sons, let alone a grandson. "How old is he?"

"Nine months."

Ethan turned back to her and reached up his free hand toward her hair. Because he loved to pull it, she always bound it tightly and high on the top of her head. But a tendril must have slipped out of the knot because he found something to yank, the fine hairs tugging on her nape. She flinched again over the jolt of pain.

Mrs. Payne chuckled. "The boys always pulled my hair, too," she said. "May I hold him?" She held out her arms as she asked, and the baby boy leaned toward her, almost falling into her embrace.

Panic flashed through Sharon at how easily he had been taken from her. That was what would happen when these people learned the truth. She would be cut out of Ethan's life as though she had never been a part of it.

"Mom." Parker drew the older woman's attention briefly from the baby she held with such awe. "Can you bring him out into the hall?" He turned toward the others. "And the rest of you leave with her. I need to talk to Ms. Wells alone."

Sharon's panic increased, making her pulse race. She lifted her arms to reach for Ethan, to take him back, but the woman was already walking out the door with the sweet baby. And Parker grabbed her outstretched arms, holding her back, as all the others left.

She hadn't really been alone with him before. She'd had Ethan. Even though he was a baby, he had been protection from Parker's wrath. He had to be furious. And he had every right to be. His son had been kept from him, and someone was trying to kill him.

But he wasn't the only one someone was trying to kill.

HOURS BEFORE, the explosion had knocked Parker on his ass, literally. Sharon Wells's announcement, that the baby was his son, had knocked him on his ass, as well, although he would have rather blamed it on the concussion. But he'd recovered quickly.

Sharon was the one trembling now, as he held her arms. A diaper bag hung heavily from one of her thin shoulders, bumping against her side. She stepped back and jerked free of his grasp; apparently she was stronger than she looked.

"I shouldn't have come here," she said. "This was a mistake…."

"Trying to pass that kid off as mine?" he asked. "That was a mistake."

And why had she done it? What had she hoped to gain? If she had been hoping to force someone to marry her, Cooper or Logan would have been the better bet; they cared more about honor than he did. But, damn his short-term memory, they were already married.

"He *is* yours," she insisted. She held his gaze, her strange light brown eyes direct and sincere. "You can get a paternity test to prove it. Since we're at the hospital, maybe they can rush the results."

He dropped his hands from her arms and stepped back. "You're serious...."

"It's just a cheek swab," she said. "It won't hurt him or else I wouldn't have suggested it."

Because she loved her son...

Their son?

He scrutinized her face. The women he usually dated wore makeup and dressed in clothes that flattered their figures. But with her enormous, unusual eyes and delicate features, she didn't really need makeup. She was actually quite beautiful. And his pulse quickened as attraction kicked in, tempting him to see just what her figure was like beneath her baggy suit.

Because of those eyes and that face and his sudden attraction to her, he knew he'd never met her before—much less been with her.

"There is no way that I am the father of *your* baby," he insisted. "I would not have forgotten you if we'd ever been intimate."

He wasn't the careless playboy everyone thought he was. He didn't have a slew of conquests whose faces he couldn't remember.

Her gaze dropped from his, and her face flushed. "But—but you have a concussion...."

He shook his head, and pain from making the motion overwhelmed him. But he kept his legs under him this time and remained conscious. And finally the confusion from the concussion receded, leaving him angry.

"There is no way that *your* child is mine."

"Take the paternity test," she urged him. "Ethan is your son."

Like everyone else, she must have believed that he was such a playboy that he wouldn't remember every woman he'd ever slept with, but his reputation was grossly exaggerated and mostly undeserved. Even with the women with whom he was involved, he always used protection. He couldn't have gotten *anyone* pregnant. So she had to be playing some angle with him, running some scheme.

Why? That paternity test she was urging him to get would only prove him right. So was she just buying some time? Was she just trying to distract him? What did she hope to gain? Did she want to collect the payout for his murder? From what Garek Kozminski had said, it sounded like a substantial amount.

Maybe he needed to search that diaper bag and make certain that she didn't have a weapon concealed. Or maybe a bomb. He reached for the strap of the bag, but his hand grazed her breast instead.

Her already enormous eyes widened with shock.

She wasn't the only one surprised. Her baggy suit hid some curves. Parker was as intrigued as he was suspicious of her.

"What—what are you doing?" she asked, her voice all breathy and anxious.

"You're trying to convince me that I made a baby with you and the concussion made me forget." No wonder she had taken the opportunity to show up now after hearing the news reports about his condition. "The effects of this concussion aren't going to last," he continued.

She nodded, either in agreement or because she was humoring him.

How far would she go to humor him? And to further whatever her agenda really was? He wanted to find out. "My memory can be jogged," he told her.

"I—I still don't understand," she stammered.

"Jog my memory," he challenged her, as he cupped her shoulders and pulled her closer.

Her eyes widened even more as she stared up at him. "Me? You want me to jog your memory?" she asked. "How?"

"Kiss me." But he didn't wait for her to take his bait; he reeled her in first. He tipped up her chin and lowered his mouth to hers.

Instead of jogging his memory, the kiss proved to him that he had never kissed her before—because it was all new. The silkiness of her lips, the warmth and sweetness of her breath as she gasped. He took advantage of that gasp to deepen the kiss, to slide his tongue inside her mouth.

His pulse raced and his head grew light again, but he didn't blame the concussion for that reaction. He blamed her. Because now she was kissing him back, her tongue sliding over his, her lips pressing against his. If her goal was just to distract him, she was doing a damn good job.

He skimmed his hands up her face to that frustrating knot on top of her head. And he tugged her hair free so that it tumbled down around her shoulders. When he had first seen her, he must have still been half-blind from the concussion. Because there was no other explanation for how he hadn't realized how beautiful she was....

She was every bit as beautiful—maybe even more beautiful—than any other woman he had ever dated. But he'd never dated her before.

It wasn't just the first kiss with her—it felt bigger than that. More monumental. It was as if the earth was shaking beneath his feet.

Or at least the building. The structure rumbled, and

the windows rattled. There were no earthquakes in Michigan—so it had to be another explosion.

Someone had set a bomb inside the hospital? Someone was so desperate to kill him that they were willing to risk the lives of more innocent people?

Of this woman? And her baby?

Smoke alarms blared, but the warning was too late. The bomb had already gone off. How many people had been hurt? And would more people be harmed trying to escape the hospital?

The commotion in the hall was so loud that it affected his throbbing head. Voices rose in fear and confusion. Footsteps pounded as if people stampeded in their panic. He glanced toward the window that had rattled. Flames reflected back from the glass. Was it too late to escape?

Or were they already trapped?

Chapter Three

The flames rose from the burning scraps of metal…of what used to be Sharon's car. She remembered where she'd parked it—between the Mini Cooper that had rolled over from the force of the blast and the SUV that was already blackened from the heat of the explosion.

She gasped as she peered out the window around Parker's broad shoulder. Her heart pounded erratically. Well, even more erratically than it had when he'd kissed her. She couldn't think about that kiss right now.

She could think only about what could have happened to Ethan and her if they had been in that car. She pressed her hand over her mouth to hold back a scream of terror. The little boy was so smart and so sweet and affectionate. His life had barely begun; it could not be lost now.

She had already determined that she would do whatever was necessary to keep him safe. But bringing him here had been a mistake. She turned away from the window and headed toward the hall.

But Parker caught her arm, stopping her. "Where do you think you're going?"

"I need to find Ethan," she said.

She needed to hold him, to make certain that the baby boy was all right. Loud noises terrified him; so did too many people, especially strangers. It was a miracle that he'd gone so willingly into Mrs. Payne's arms, but that had been before the explosion and the chaos.

"I need to be with—"

"Here he is," Mrs. Payne said as she walked back into the room with her grandson.

Just as Sharon had feared, he was crying. Tears streamed down his chubby cheeks. His screams must have escalated to hysteria because all he was doing now was gasping for shaky breaths.

She reached for him, and he nearly leaped into her arms, snuggling into her neck. His hands clutched her hair, pulling it around him. And she didn't even care. Her eyes stung with tears at the thought of losing him. She loved this little boy so much; she couldn't love him any more if he was actually hers.

"IT WAS HERS." Logan confirmed what Parker had already suspected when he'd realized that the explosion had been a car in the parking lot blowing up.

At least it hadn't been inside the hospital or close enough to the building to cause any structural damage. The windows had rattled and the floor had shaken, and the smoke from the parking lot had set off some of the alarms.

Logan added, "And the kid is yours."

Stunned, Parker tensed and paused with his hand on his gun. That baby was his? But that made no sense. Unless…

Like a hostage at a bank holdup, Logan lifted his arms. "Don't shoot me. I'm just the messenger."

Parker slid his gun into the holster he had strapped under his arm. God, it felt good to be out of that hospital gown. And in a few minutes, he would be out of the hospital, too. After the explosion in the parking lot and all the media trying to get past security, he doubted that the doctor would protest his leaving early.

"The tests came back already?" he asked as he tried to slow the rapid beat of his heart.

It had been just as she'd said—just a simple cheek swab. From the baby. And him. And Logan and Cooper.

"Mom sweet-talked someone in the lab into rushing the results," Logan replied.

Only a couple of hours had passed since the car exploded. The paternity test had been taken before the police arrived to talk to them. An officer had taken Sharon into a separate room, no doubt to question why and when someone would have put a bomb on her car. The police would have run the registration or vehicle number, if nothing had been left of the plate, to find out who owned it.

Parker had wanted to hear Sharon's answers, too. But those weren't the only answers he wanted from Sharon Wells.

"So who is she?" Logan asked.

"I have no idea," he replied honestly.

Logan gestured around the hospital room. "It's just you and me, Park. Tell me the truth."

"I have no idea," he repeated.

"So she was just a one-night stand?"

His temper rising, Parker grabbed the front of his twin's shirt. "She's not a one-night stand." Not his, and he doubted, from the innocent way she dressed, that she was anyone else's. He just wished he knew what exactly she was. A con artist? A killer? A kidnapper?

He hoped like hell she was none of those things. But

he couldn't let the sweetness of her kiss alleviate his suspicions about her.

"But you don't even know who she is," Logan pointed out.

"I'm going to change that," he said. When the police were done with her, he was going to take his turn interrogating her. Hopefully he hadn't lost his touch from his years with the River City Police Department. Of course, he had spent more time undercover than interrogating suspects. That had been more Logan's job, which he was proving with his inquisition of him.

"Since you've got a baby together, that would probably be a good thing," Logan remarked. He shook his head. "I can't believe you're a father...."

Neither could Parker. But he had no reason to doubt the test. The only one he doubted was Sharon Wells.

THIS HAD BEEN a mistake. Sharon had realized that even before Parker Payne had kissed her. She should not have come here. But she had been warned to trust no one else. So she hadn't told the police anything—not that she'd had much to tell them. She really had no idea who was trying to kill her or why. But she hadn't told the officers about the other attempts on her life.

And she had tried to pass this one off as her car being mistaken for someone else's—maybe even Parker Payne's. He was the one who someone was trying to kill—or so the news reports had claimed.

The gray-haired police officer opened the door of the vacant doctor's office he had used to question her and held it for her. She had her hands full with the diaper bag and the sleeping baby. Ethan had exhausted himself from crying, but even in slumber, he clung to her, strands of her hair clutched in his chubby little fists.

How could she love this child so much? He had never been part of her plan. She had never wanted to marry or have children; she had intended to focus only on her career.

"You're very lucky, miss," the officer told her.

How? Along with her car, Sharon had lost her purse and her suitcases. She sighed. "I know it was just a vehicle..."

She could replace the money and other lost items; she would not have been able to replace Ethan. But even though he hadn't been hurt in the explosion, she was still going to lose him.

To his father...

"The car wasn't the only thing lost," the officer informed her. "The bomb didn't go off until someone started the engine."

"But I had the keys," she murmured. But when she patted the pocket on the front of the diaper bag, she realized they weren't there. She must have left them dangling from the ignition.

"Security cameras picked up someone checking out cars in the lot, obviously looking for one to steal," the officer said.

"Someone was trying to steal my car?" Because she had left the keys and the purse and the suitcases...

How had she been so careless? She'd had her hands full with Ethan. But she'd also been scared to bring Parker Payne a baby he hadn't even known he had.

Shaking his head as if in pity of the dead carjacker, the officer said, "He picked the wrong car to steal."

And he'd died because of it—because of *her.* She

gasped as guilt and regret overwhelmed her. But then a strong hand gripped her shoulder, squeezing gently as if offering reassurance.

She glanced up at Parker Payne. He was dressed in a shirt nearly as blue as his brilliant eyes; it was tucked into a pair of faded jeans. She kind of missed the hospital gown.

"Did the security cameras pick up who planted the bomb?" Parker asked the officer.

The older man shook his head again with regret. "The bomber knew where the cameras were and avoided them. We're going to have the techs go over the footage again to see if they can find anything usable."

Parker nodded in approval.

She was surprised the officer had been so free with information about a police investigation. But then the older man clasped Parker's shoulder.

"Glad you're alive, Payne," he said. "Losing your father was hard enough."

A muscle twitched along Parker's clenched jaw, and he nodded again.

"You tired of working for your brother yet?" he asked. "We'd love to have you back on the force."

Parker arched a brow as if in skepticism of the older man's claim.

"Well, maybe not now," the officer amended, "but once you find out who's trying to kill you..."

"That'll be soon," Parker promised.

"We'll help," the officer said. He turned to Sharon. "But until that person is caught, you might want to stay away from Mr. Payne, miss. For your own safety..."

She had already discovered she wasn't safe anywhere, either.

"We'll protect her, too," Parker said. "It's what Payne Protection does."

His family ran a security firm; he acted as a bodyguard. But what happened when he was the one needing protection? Who protected him?

He stepped back to allow the officer to pass him, and she saw the others standing just down the hall. The brothers who looked so much like him and the other two men who looked like each other with their blond hair and light-colored eyes. All of the men watched him and her carefully, as if they didn't even trust *her* not to try to kill him.

But then, they were smart to trust no one—especially not her. She needed to tell him the truth. But when she turned back to him and found him staring in wonder at the sleeping baby she held, she realized that he already knew.

"He is your son," she said.

"I know." But he shook his head as if he was still in denial of being a dad. Or maybe that wasn't what he was denying....

He was denying *her*.

Pain clutched her heart, and even though it killed her to admit it, she added, "I am not his mother."

"I know."

Of course he knew. Despite the concussion, he would have remembered her had they ever been involved. But they would have never been involved. Even when they'd previously met, they hadn't been formally introduced; they had only glanced at each other in passing. Apparently he hadn't noticed her, but she had noticed him. It was impossible to not notice a man as devastatingly handsome and charming as Parker Payne.

But he wasn't her type any more than she was his. She would never have gone for a man with his reputation or with his good looks. The only men she had ever dated, and there had been only a few, had been as serious about their education and their careers as she had been.

Before her little man had come along. Before Ethan...

So what was she supposed to do now? Hand Parker Payne his son and walk away? That was what she had been instructed to do, but her car was gone now. Her purse and money, too. She had no means with which to walk away...even if she could bring herself to turn her little man over to strangers.

"You're coming with me," he told her, as if he had read her mind or, more likely, seen her indecision. "And you're going to tell me what the hell is going on...."

If only she knew...

But just as she hadn't immediately admitted that she wasn't Ethan's mother, she stalled on admitting her ignorance, too. She needed more time with the little boy—enough time to make sure he would be safe...without her.

Parker's hand moved to her elbow now, as he guided her toward his family and friends. "We need a diversion," he told them, "a way to get out of here and make sure that no one follows us."

One of his brothers nodded. "We'll distract whoever might be watching. Do you have a safe place to take them?"

Parker nodded.

But Sharon felt no relief. Parker might be able to keep them safe from whoever was after them. But who would keep her safe from him?

One of the light-haired men spoke. "I found out more information from my contacts."

Parker lifted a brow in question. "You know who ordered the hit on me?"

He shook his head. "No, but I know that you're not the only one. A hit was put out on someone else the same day as it was put out on you."

His eyes darkening with concern, Parker glanced toward his brother.

And the man shook his head again. "It's on a woman." His gray-eyed gaze focused on her. "A woman named Sharon Wells."

So she hadn't just been in the wrong places at the wrong times. It had not been coincidence or mistaken identity. Someone was definitely trying to kill *her.* Someone wanted both her and Parker Payne dead.

Chapter Four

Parker closed and locked the door behind Sharon Wells and the baby she carried—his baby. Then he slid his gun back into the holster beneath his shoulder. Before he'd brought her up from the garage in the basement, he had cleared the penthouse condo on Lake Michigan that his brother Logan used as a safe house. Parker had also made certain they weren't followed from the hospital.

"We'll be safe here," he assured her.

She trembled—maybe with cold or maybe with exhaustion from carrying the sleeping child. When he'd cleared the penthouse, he had also brought up the portable crib his mother had somehow conjured up at the hospital. He had set it up in a corner of the master bedroom. He reached out for the baby and carefully lifted him from her arms. But the child—even in his sleep—clutched her hair in his hands, binding the baby to her as if those tresses were caramel-colored ropes.

She was not his mother; she had finally admitted that. But there was definitely a bond between her and the baby. She gently pried open the little fingers so that her hair slipped free. And Parker held only the baby.

Ethan—she called him. His son's name was Ethan. He stared down in wonder at the little boy. His pudgy cheeks were flushed and drool trailed from the corner of his open mouth. His fuzzy black hair was damp, too. He had been held so tightly in Sharon's arms that the child had gotten too warm. She had held him as if she would never let him go. And now she visibly held her breath as she watched him handle the baby, as if afraid that Parker might drop him.

That he might hurt him…

A test had proved that somehow this child was his. Parker had vowed to never become a father, but now that he was, he would do anything for his son. He would die for him before he would ever let any harm come to him.

If Ethan had been in that car when it exploded…

Parker shuddered in horror over the thought. He could have lost his child before he had ever realized that the little boy was his. He never wanted to let him go now, but the little boy was already overly warm. And Parker was hot himself—with anger over Sharon Wells's deception. But she watched him as if he was the one who couldn't be trusted.

Very gently, so that he didn't awaken the boy, he laid him down in the crib. The child sighed softly as he relaxed against the thin mattress, his slumber deepening.

"We're safe here," he repeated. But he was reassuring himself now that nothing would happen to his little boy.

"You probably want to kill me yourself," she said, "for misleading you."

He snorted. "Misleading me?" He wrapped his fingers around her arm and tugged her farther from the crib so that he wouldn't wake the baby as the anger he had barely been able to contain boiled over in his voice. "That's all you think you've done?"

"I didn't lie to you," she insisted, those huge light

brown eyes wide with innocence and sincerity. "I never told you that I was Ethan's mother—just that you are his father."

He dropped his hand from her arm as he realized she hadn't lied. She had never claimed to be the baby's mother; he had only assumed that she was because she had brought the baby to him. Why hadn't the boy's mother? That woman—whoever she was—had kept her pregnancy from him.

"Why were you the one to bring me my son?" he wondered aloud.

While the baby's mother hadn't even told him that he was a father, this woman had brought him his baby. She had shared a secret that wasn't even hers.

"I shouldn't be mad at you," he said as he turned back to the crib and studied the sleeping baby. "I should probably be thanking you instead." If not for Sharon Wells, he might never have known he had a son.

"So you don't want to kill me?" she asked, but she narrowed those eyes with suspicion as if she still couldn't trust him. But given that someone was trying to kill them, she shouldn't trust him or anyone else.

He shrugged. "I don't know." He was treating her as his family treated each other, making jokes to defuse a tense situation. "I could use the money for carrying out the hit. Maybe set up a college fund for Ethan…"

She smiled nervously, probably not completely certain he was kidding.

He wasn't entirely kidding. He would have to set up a college fund; he would have to provide for his son's present and his future. But he wouldn't be able to do any of that if he was dead.

And why was there a hit out on Sharon, as well? She wasn't the baby's mother, so who exactly was she?

"Maybe you haven't lied to me," he said, "but you haven't been completely honest with me, either. You know a lot more than I do. You know who Ethan's mother is."

Color flushed her face, giving away her guilt.

"And I think you even know why someone's trying to kill us," he continued, "maybe even who…"

She shook her head and all that thick hair tumbled around her shoulders. He was so glad that he had pulled it free from that knot. Those caramel-colored waves softened the sharp angles of her thin face, making her beautiful. "I don't know why," she said, "or who…"

He stared into her eyes, trying to gauge if she was being honest. If only he were the interrogator that his brother, the former detective, was…

But he had been the undercover cop—the one more adept at keeping secrets than at flushing them out. He hadn't needed confessions; he had caught 'em in the act—in the commission of the crime.

Had Sharon Wells committed any crime?

"Who are you?" he asked.

It wasn't the question he should be asking. He should be asking who Ethan's mother was. But Sharon was the one with the bounty on her head—not whoever the baby's mother was. And for some reason Parker was more interested in Sharon than in whoever had kept his son from him.

"Who are you?" Parker asked again.

SHARON HAD EXPECTED his anger. She hadn't expected his suspicion. "I told you who I am. I would show you my driver's license to prove it, but it burned up when my car exploded."

But more than material possessions had blown up. Somebody had lost his life because of her, because someone else wanted her dead. And that man might not have been the only one who'd been hurt in the cross fire....

Parker crossed the enormous master suite to a desk near the window that overlooked Lake Michigan. The sun was setting now, streaking across the surface of the water. He lifted a piece of paper from a fax machine. "Here's a copy of your license."

Her face—looking pale and tense—stared back at her from the paper he held up. Then he replaced that with another photo—one of a burned-out and boarded-up apartment building. "And here's a picture of the address on your driver's license...."

Sharon stepped closer to him. "Did anyone die in the fire?" She reached for the picture, which was actually part of a newspaper article.

He caught her wrist. "You knew about this?" A muscle twitched in his cheek and his blue eyes were so intense, so filled with concern. "Were you and Ethan there when the building caught fire?"

His concern was for his son. But she was concerned for the baby, too. She had been entrusted with his safety, with his welfare. It wasn't a job for which she had asked, but it was one she had taken more seriously than her *real* job. And she had nearly failed. She glanced at that picture of destruction and shuddered.

"No," she replied. "We weren't there. But I saw it on the news."

Panic clutched her heart as she remembered that horrific moment when she had realized that it was her home on the news, her apartment complex burning, flames reflecting off the shattered glass on the blackened lawn.

"I know there were injuries," she said, "but I haven't seen any follow-up reports to see if everyone recovered."

That muscle twitched in his cheek again and he replied slowly, with reluctance, "Someone was killed…."

She sucked in a breath. "That's two people," she murmured. "Two people killed because of me…."

"Today two people were killed because of *me.*" He slid his hand from her wrist up her arm and squeezed her shoulder, offering comfort and sharing her guilt. "Two friends—two family men—lost their lives because someone wanted *me* dead."

Tears stung her eyes, but she blinked them back. Long ago she had learned that crying was a waste of time. And she had never had anyone offer her a shoulder to cry on or arms to hold her. She had been left alone with swollen eyes and a red face.

"Why does someone want you dead?" he asked and then repeated his question again. "Who *are* you?"

"You have a copy of my license. You know who I am."

He shook his head. "I know your name and your old address. But that doesn't tell me why someone would want you dead. Are you involved with the wrong people?"

She hadn't thought so…until now.

"Do you have a crazy boyfriend?" he asked, firing questions at her like bullets. "A dangerous career? Do you lead a life of crime?"

She laughed at the wild image he painted of her. It could not have been further from the truth. He had to have been kidding again like he had when he'd acted as if he would consider killing her for the money.

From the little time she had spent around his family, she had noticed that they teased each other as a way of communicating. But what did she know about family? She had never really had one.

"You think this is funny?" he asked, his voice gruff with disapproval.

"Of course I don't," she said. With all the guilt and fear she felt, she was barely holding it together. If she let herself think about those people…

Tears stung her eyes, but she blinked them back. If she gave in to them, she wouldn't be able to stop. "I think this is surreal. None of this is my life. None of this has anything to do with me. I am only the messenger delivering your son."

He laughed bitterly. "You make yourself sound like FedEx, like you're just delivering a package."

That was what she had been told—how the baby had been referred to—as a package. She cringed now as she remembered Ethan's mother's careless words.

"And that's bull," he said, "because you have an undeniable bond with…" His throat moved as if emotion choked him. He visibly swallowed and continued. "…my son."

He had already claimed his child. Where did that leave Sharon? If she admitted everything to him, it would leave her alone again as she already had been for so much of her life. But she shrugged off the self-pity and focused on what was important: Ethan would have a parent who would love and protect him.

And if Parker were to protect his son, he had to find out who was trying to kill him and stop that person. So she had to tell him everything she knew—the little that it was.

"I have been taking care of him," she said, "pretty much since he's been born."

"You're a foster mother?" he asked.

She shook her head.

"A nanny?"

She sighed. That wasn't the job she had started out with, but it was the one she had wound up doing. "I'm a law student."

"So you work as a nanny on the side?"

"I work as a law clerk for a judge." And she watched realization dawn on his handsome face. He knew who the mother of his son was.

He cursed. But then he tensed and glanced toward his son, as if regretful of swearing in front of the child. Ethan slept on, though. "Judge Foster?"

He had slept with the woman but didn't address her by her first name?

She nodded.

And he shook his head. "She told me that she couldn't have kids…."

"She was actually having fertility treatments so that she could," Sharon said, flinching as she remembered the judge's mercurial mood changes. She had been so thrilled to get the position clerking for the infamous Judge Brenda Foster…until she'd actually had the job. But the job as clerk had turned into the nanny job when Brenda had been unable to keep any other nannies working for her.

He cursed again but under his breath. "I need to talk to her."

"Good luck," she murmured. "I haven't been able to reach her for the past two weeks."

"Two weeks?" he echoed in shock. "She hasn't seen her child in two weeks?"

With all the hours the judge worked and socialized, two weeks wasn't the longest she had gone without seeing her son. "She sent me and Ethan away with enough cash to stay in hotels for two weeks. She didn't want me using credit cards to buy anything."

"Because she didn't want you to get tracked down," Parker said, his blue eyes narrowing. "She must have known someone was after you."

Sharon shook her head. "Nobody was after me."

He clutched the paper in his hand so tightly that he crumpled it. "This newspaper article proves otherwise. And so does your car getting blown up in the hospital parking lot today."

Sharon shuddered as she faced the reality that someone definitely wanted her dead. Why?

"What else did the judge tell you?" Parker asked.

Sharon sighed. "Just that if I hadn't heard from her before those two weeks were over, I was to bring Ethan to you." It wasn't exactly what the judge had said, but he was already so angry with Brenda—and rightfully so—that Sharon didn't want to make the situation worse.

But then, she wasn't certain that it could get much worse…until she heard the creak of footsteps on the stairs. Parker heard them, too, because he reached for his gun. Obviously, he hadn't been expecting anyone.

He had promised that they would be safe here. But Sharon was beginning to fear that they wouldn't be safe anywhere—not with someone determined that they die.

The steps squeaked again. There was more than one person coming up the stairwell. While Parker was armed, he was outnumbered. And even if he had another gun,

Sharon had never touched one, let alone knew how to use one. She could only watch helplessly as he moved toward the stairs—putting himself between her and Ethan and the threat to all their lives….

Chapter Five

Curses echoed inside Parker's head. He had been so certain that he hadn't been followed. He'd been so certain that he had done everything necessary to keep his son and Sharon Wells safe. He hadn't even told his family where he was bringing them, just that he had a place.

As a head rose above the stairwell railing, the curses slipped through his lips. "Damn you, Logan! I could've shot you…." His twin had admonished him many times for sneaking up on him. Why hadn't the lesson applied to himself?

"I wasn't sure if you knew about this place," Logan said. "But Mom was insistent that I find you."

And her head rose above the stairwell railing as she pushed past her oldest and rushed over to the youngest Payne. The new grandmother uttered a wistful sigh as she stared down at the sleeping baby.

She had known about her grandchild for only a few hours, but it was obvious she already loved him. Something gripped Parker's heart, squeezing it tightly, and he realized he loved the baby, too. Ethan was a part of him.

And a part of Brenda Foster. She had lied to him. She had tricked him. Those tactics had made her such an effective district attorney that she had been one of the youngest judges ever appointed to the bench. And her ruthlessness had made her both one of the most respected and most hated judges ever.

Parker had been flattered that such a successful woman had been attracted to him. But while he'd been her bodyguard, he had refused to act anything but professional with her. So she'd fired Payne Protection. He had been attracted to her combination of beauty and brains, and once he no longer worked for her, he had acted on that attraction.

And, unbeknownst to him, they had created a child. She hadn't just lied to him once; she had continued that lie with every day she had kept his baby's existence from him. What had compelled her to finally have Sharon Wells bring the baby to him?

What kind of trouble was she in? Because of her ruthlessness as a judge, she had made many enemies and had constantly received threats to her life. But why would those criminals threaten the life of the father of her child and her nanny?

"I'm actually glad you showed up," Parker begrudgingly admitted to his overprotective twin.

"What?" Logan reached for his gun and glanced around the condo as if looking for intruders hiding in the shadows. "Were you followed?"

"No. I was careful." If he hadn't been, he and Sharon would already be dead. "But I need to leave for a while. I need to go see someone."

And find out what kind of game she was playing....

This was about more than a criminal with a grudge or the hit would have been on Brenda. Not on her nanny and the father of her child.

"So I need you to protect Sharon and...my son...." He could say those words that he thought he would never say because he couldn't *not* claim that beautiful little boy as his. Like his mother, he already loved the child. "I need you to protect them while I'm gone."

"Where are you going?" Logan asked.

Sharon just stared at him because she obviously knew where. She knew that he would have to go to Brenda. He would have to see her and maybe have a few choice words with her.... He couldn't believe how she had lied and tricked him and cheated him out of Ethan's first months of life.

"I'm going to see Judge Foster," he admitted. "She's part of this whole mess." He wasn't going to share that she was also a part of Ethan. He wouldn't share that news with his family until he talked to the judge herself.

"Judge Foster fired us over a year and a half ago," Logan recalled. "What would she have to do with anything going on with you and Sharon?"

"I work for her," Sharon said. But like him, she didn't divulge any more information. Maybe she was following his lead; maybe she didn't want his family to know that Ethan wasn't her son.

Logan dragged his hand through his hair in frustration and warned him, "You can't just go traipsing off alone when you've got a bounty on your head."

"I'll be fine," Parker assured him. "Nobody's touched me yet." Not for lack of trying, though.

"He won't be alone," Sharon said. "I'm going with him."

Parker shook his head. "Nobody's touched me," he repeated. "But a lot of other people got hurt or worse because they were too close to me."

So there was no way he would let her go along, no way that he would put Sharon Wells in any more danger than she already was.

SHARON SHOULDN'T HAVE left the baby…because she worried that she might never see him again. But at least she knew that he had a family—a real family. They would protect him and take care of him—not out of obligation but love.

Mrs. Payne had clearly fallen for her grandson. He wasn't an inconvenience for her. Or evidence of her son's mistake.

That was all Sharon had been to her grandparents—proof of their perfect daughter's fall from grace. The mistake that had ruined and eventually claimed her life. After Sharon's young mother had died, they'd taken over responsibility for raising her. Not out of love but out of fear that their friends and colleagues would think less of them if they had given her up for adoption like they had once urged their daughter to do. Even if she hadn't overheard their heated debate about whether or not to keep her, she would have figured out how they'd felt about her.

"You should have stayed with Ethan," Parker said as if he'd read her mind. Or maybe he had seen the fear and doubt on her face.

But darkness had fallen. And he had shut off the car so not even the dash lights illuminated the interior. He had also parked down the street from the judge's house but put some distance between the car and the lamps that burned outside the gates.

Then he admonished himself. "I shouldn't have brought you here."

"You had to," she reminded him, "or you wouldn't

have gotten past the security system." He had tried calling the judge, but she hadn't answered any of her phones, not the one at the house or her office or her cell. Brenda either wasn't home or wasn't in any condition to let them in. Panic pressed on Sharon's lungs. What if something had happened to Ethan's mother?

He had family that would take care of him. But Sharon had taken care of him for the judge; the Paynes wouldn't need her help like Brenda had. She would no longer have any connection to the child she had come to love as if he was her own.

Parker groaned. "That damn security system..."

Payne Protection had installed the high-tech system that didn't use codes but fingerprint recognition. Sharon was surprised that Parker's print wasn't able to deactivate it. But then, Brenda hadn't wanted him to have access to her house because she hadn't wanted him to know about his son.

She had wanted a child but no husband. No family. While Sharon respected the woman, she hadn't understood her desire for a baby. All Sharon had ever wanted was a career—one as successful as Judge Foster's. But then she'd met Ethan and had fallen for him.

"I still shouldn't have brought you," Parker said.

"You would have had to cut off my finger, then." She shuddered at the repulsive thought.

Parker chuckled. "I think my brother's new in-laws might be able to find a less gruesome way to bypass it. I doubt there's a security system that a Kozminski can't compromise."

"But they would need time to do that, and I haven't heard from the judge in two weeks," Sharon reminded him.

"And that's out of the ordinary for her?" he asked.

Not wanting to criticize the judge, she hesitated. "She's always very busy. But usually she would just have me take Ethan back to my place if she wanted us out of the way. But this time she wanted us out of town for those two weeks," she reminded him in case he still suffered short-term memory loss, "and she wanted me to use cash for everything—for the hotel and for food."

"She didn't want anyone to be able to track you down," Parker said. "She was hiding you and Ethan. So she must have known you were in danger."

Sharon shook her head. "I wasn't in danger before those two weeks. I wasn't the reason that she sent me and Ethan away."

"But you work for her and she is always in danger," Parker said. "You could have gotten caught in the cross fire."

"I'm kind of invisible. People don't usually notice me." Ignoring the sting to her pride, she admitted, "You obviously didn't notice me since you keep claiming to have never seen me before."

"I claimed to not have slept with you," he clarified, "which is true."

Maybe it was true, but he made it sound impossible. Of course, it probably was. "And that you never saw me before, and that's not true."

"When didn't I notice you?" he asked.

"When you were Brenda's bodyguard," she said. "I was working in her office then." Even then she had done little law clerking and more coffee- and lunch-getting. "I saw you a few times." Those times had admittedly been brief, but his ridiculously handsome image had lingered in her mind.

His eyes glinted in the darkness as he stared at her. "No, I would have remembered...."

"Maybe it's the concussion," she said. But she knew it was her being unremarkable. She had learned long ago to be unobtrusive and quiet, but she'd still felt like such an inconvenience and disappointment to her grandparents.

He touched his head. "Maybe the concussion is why I brought you with me when I should have left you with Logan for protection."

"And you would get into the estate...how?" she wondered.

"The Kozminskis..."

"Won't be able to deactivate the system that quickly," she pointed out. "Do you really want to wait any longer to talk to her?"

Even in the darkness, she noticed the muscle twitch in his cheek. He had to be furious with Brenda for having tricked him into helping her conceive Ethan and then for keeping the little boy from him.

His voice was gruff when he replied. "No."

Then he opened the driver's door. He had done something to the dome light because it didn't come on, leaving her in the darkness.

She fumbled for the handle on her side, but as she did, the door opened. He wrapped his fingers around her arm and helped her from the car.

"I'm taking you with me," he said. "But you need to stay close to me."

Her breath caught at his words. She had no problem sticking close to his side—for warmth and protection. His tall, muscular body blocked some of the cold wind that whipped at her loose hair and penetrated the thin material of her suit. And his gun, clutched tightly in his free hand, offered some security as fear chilled Sharon even more than the wind.

Sharon was tall but she had to quicken her pace to match Parker's long strides down the street. As they stopped at the gate, she drew in a quick breath before reaching for the security panel. But Parker caught her hand, holding her back from touching it.

"What's wrong?" she asked. Her skin tingled and warmed from the contact with his. He didn't let her go, continuing to hold her hand.

Didn't he want to go inside? Hadn't that been the point of coming to Brenda's estate?

Parker glanced around the area, his gaze scanning the street before he peered through the wrought-iron gate at the dark mansion on the other side.

"I wish I had Cujo," he murmured.

"Cujo?" Just how badly had he been concussed that he was longing for a fictional dog?

"My sister-in-law's former K9 German shepherd," he explained. "He's great at sniffing out bombs."

"You think there could be one inside?" she asked, turning her attention to that large brick residence. "But nobody could have gotten past security."

He studied the panel now, as if trying to determine if it had been tampered with. Still holding her hand, he lifted it toward the panel.

She pressed her index finger to the glass. A light flashed as the machine read her print. The lock clicked, then a motor revved and metal rattled as the gate drew open. Parker stepped inside but held Sharon back with a hand on her shoulder.

"You can't leave me out here!" she said, her voice cracking with fear as she imagined being alone in the dark.

It brought back memories of another lonely night long ago. She had been in the dark that night, hidden away. She reached out and clutched his arm.

"Don't leave me!" She had said the same thing that night but she had been too late. "You need me to open the house door, too."

"I won't leave you here," he assured her. "But you have to be careful. We don't know what we're going to find inside."

Her stomach muscles tightened with fear and dread. "You think she's dead?"

"It would have been on the news," he said, "if the judge had been killed or even if she'd gone missing."

She shook her head. "She had taken a leave of absence from work."

"Brenda Foster?" he asked, obviously incredulous.

He wasn't the only one who had been surprised. Brenda had taken only a couple weeks off after having Ethan.

"I think she was writing her memoirs or some kind of book," Sharon said. "She told me that I would have to do some proofreading for her when she was ready. But she hadn't asked me to look at anything yet."

"How long had she been off work?" he asked.

"Her leave started two weeks ago," Sharon said, "so nobody at the courts would have been alarmed that they hadn't heard from her."

"Would anyone else?"

"Are you asking me about her boyfriends or lovers?" Irritation eased some of her fear. He had kissed her, but now he was questioning her about another woman's social life. Of course, he had only kissed Sharon to prove the point that she couldn't be the mother of his child and not because he had actually been attracted or interested in her enough to want to kiss her.

"I'm asking if anyone would have reported her missing if they hadn't heard from her."

Guilt clutched her at the realization that she had been so petty as to be jealous of another woman—a woman she had always respected. But Sharon was one of very few who'd actually been close to the judge. "I don't know...."

She didn't know who would report *her* missing, either. With the hours she worked, she had little time to socialize. Not that she had ever socialized much. She had been more focused on school and studying and work than on making friends.

"Probably me," she said. As Ethan's primary caregiver, she was closer to his mother than anyone else. "But she told me to go to you if I didn't hear from her—and to trust no one else."

"Not even the police?"

She shrugged and then shivered. "No one but you."

Parker turned back toward the mansion. He cursed and reluctantly admitted, "I should have let Logan send backup with me."

"But there's no hit out on Brenda," she reminded him. "There is no reason to think anyone's trying to kill her."

"There isn't," he agreed. "But I know that someone's trying to kill us."

"They don't know that we would come here," she said. "And you made sure we weren't followed."

"So I could leave you out here...."

"You need me to open the door," she reminded him.

So she got that far with him—to the massive double front doors. After she pressed her index finger to the security panel, they opened slowly and creepily as if a ghost played butler for them.

Parker stepped over the threshold first, his gun drawn. He'd turned on a flashlight that was attached to the barrel, which he swung in every direction he turned, as if ready to confront a threat. But the house was eerily quiet. He must have thought so, too, because he asked, "Doesn't she have *any* live-in staff?"

"No." She wanted Sharon on call 24/7 but she hadn't wanted her to live with her. "She prefers her privacy, so she just has a cleaning service."

But that had obviously been canceled because as they crossed the foyer, it was clear that no one had been in to straighten up. Brenda's stilettos had been abandoned on the marble floor and her coat lay a little farther inside the house at the foot of the double stairwell leading to the second story. Parker lifted his foot to the first step, but Sharon grasped his arm.

"She won't be up there."

"But it's late and all the lights are off."

Brenda wouldn't have been in bed yet, though, unless she had company, and in that case, there would have been lights on. "She would be working," she said, and she started across the expansive living room toward the double doors that led to the den.

But Parker caught her arm, jerking her aside before she could reach for the door handles. He swung the beam of the flashlight around the doors.

"What are you looking for?" she asked.

"Trip wires—anything that could trigger a bomb."

She shuddered.

"It's clear," he said.

But she didn't reach for the handle again, so he had to turn it. He pushed open the doors and swung the beam around the room. It glanced off books and papers. But they weren't on the bookshelf or the desk. They were strewn across the floor.

"Someone's ransacked the room," he said.

She shook her head. "No. Her chambers often look like this." Each of the books was open to a specific page. But as she stepped inside the room with Parker, she noted that these books were ripped apart.

"Someone was looking for something," he said. "Can you tell if anything's missing?"

"Her laptop." It wasn't on the desk or the floor in front of it.

"She must have taken it with her," Parker said. "She must have taken off."

Sharon stepped carefully over the books and papers to move around to the back of the big mahogany desk. If Brenda had taken the laptop, she would have put it in the case that she usually dropped behind her chair.

But she didn't find the bag behind the desk. She found something else instead—something she wished she had never seen. As she gave in to the fear and hysteria overwhelming her, screams burned her throat.

Chapter Six

Parker had known he shouldn't have brought Sharon along with him. But since there wasn't a hit out on Brenda, he hadn't thought they would be in danger in her mansion—as long as he made certain that they weren't followed. Now he knew why there was no hit on the judge.

She was already dead. On the floor behind her desk, her body sprawled across the toppled-over leather chair. Her neck was bent at an odd angle—not because of how she was lying but because her neck had been broken. Blood, trailing from her mouth, had dried into a thick, black pool beneath her head. Her face was ghostly white. She must have been dead for a while. It could have been days, or weeks....

Sharon trembled and shivered in his arms. She was in shock.

But at least she had finally stopped screaming. Her voice had grown hoarse and cracked before she had finally calmed down, before she had finally stopped punching her fists into his chest and collapsed against him.

He shouldn't have brought her here. He should have known it was a possibility that they might find the judge dead. But he was more surprised by what they hadn't found. Her bodyguard. While Brenda might not have let any other staff stay overnight, she would have kept the bodyguard—especially since she must have been aware that she was in danger.

Why else had she sent the baby away with Sharon? She must have loved her son—*their* son. Maybe Brenda Foster hadn't been as manipulative and selfish a woman as he had once thought she was. She had tricked and lied to him, but as long as she'd loved their son…

"I'm sorry," Sharon murmured, as she clutched at his shirt, which was damp from her tears. "So sorry…"

Why was she apologizing?

"I'm the one who should be sorry," he said. "And I am. I shouldn't have brought you here. You shouldn't have had to see your boss like this…."

She drew in a shuddery breath, fighting back more sobs. "But she was the mother of your son." Her voice cracked and the tears began to fall again. "Ethan…"

His son no longer had a mother. And the boy's father had been aware of him for only hours….

Now Parker was solely responsible for him? He had no idea how to take care of a baby, how to be a father. A twinge of panic struck his heart, but he ignored it. He would figure it out—with his family's help. So he pushed aside that worry and focused on the woman trembling in his arms. He had to be strong for her.

But instead of clinging to him, she began to tense and ease away from him.

"Are you all right?" he asked Sharon. "I need to make some calls."

She nodded and pulled completely away from him. Replacing his arms with hers, she wrapped them around herself—as if trying to hold herself together. "Of course. You have to call the police."

She must have noticed his hesitation because she gasped and asked, “You are calling the police, right?”

He wasn’t sure that he should and reminded Sharon, “Brenda told you to trust nobody but me.”

Those already enormous eyes widened as if she was scared that she had trusted the wrong man. “B-but you can’t just leave her here like this….”

Brenda Foster was beyond help. It was Sharon and Ethan about whom he was concerned. But the crime scene needed to be processed for evidence. So he reached for his phone. But his first call wasn’t to the police.

He had called a woman—a beautiful, young woman with auburn hair and brown eyes. She showed up before the police arrived. But he didn’t let her look at the body; he didn’t even let her past the security-system control panel at the door to the den.

And goose bumps rose on Sharon’s skin beneath the thin material of her jacket. What if Brenda had been wrong about him? What if she shouldn’t have trusted Parker Payne?

“Are you all right?” the woman asked Sharon, her brown eyes warm with concern.

Sharon must have looked as pale and sick as she felt. Seeing Brenda like that… It had brought back so many horrific memories that she had lost it. And she was barely hanging on to her composure now. She could only nod.

The woman turned toward Parker. “Did you call an ambulance?”

Parker glanced up from where he was studying the body—that horribly broken and lifeless body—behind the desk. “She’s been beyond medical help for a while now.”

“I’m not talking about the judge….” She gestured toward Sharon.

"I'm—I'm okay," she insisted. "I don't need an ambulance."

"She's in shock." The woman spoke again to Parker, as if Sharon wasn't even in the room.

Who were they to each other? Obviously the brunette worked in the security business, too, since she hooked a laptop to the security panel at the door, so familiar with the high-tech system that she must have handled it all the time.

Parker moved from behind the desk to join the woman at the door. But she didn't look at him; she was focused on the laptop instead. How could she ignore Parker Payne? How could any woman? He turned toward Sharon and studied her face. "Are you really all right?"

She nodded again. Physically, she was fine. Emotionally, she was a mess. But it wasn't just over finding another dead body. It was over the suspicion that had begun to niggle at her.

Why had Parker called this woman to mess with the security system? To cover his tracks?

And Sharon had left Ethan with his family. If Parker couldn't be trusted, could she trust any of the Paynes?

"I—I should get back to Ethan," she said. "He'll be afraid if he wakes up and I'm not there."

"Ethan?" The young woman's breath caught, and she stared at Sharon. "Is that…your baby's name?"

Parker hadn't told anyone that Sharon wasn't the boy's mother; he had told them only that he had to talk to the judge, for whom Sharon worked. He hadn't told them the reason *specifically,* only that Judge Foster might have some involvement or information about why someone wanted him and Sharon dead.

Judge Foster couldn't help them now. Not when she had already become a victim….

But whose victim?

"Ethan is my son," Parker told the woman. "You could have met him at the hospital if you'd been there…."

If they meant anything to each other, why hadn't she been at the hospital when he had been wounded in that explosion? He was obviously hurt that she hadn't come to see him, so this woman was important to him.

If Sharon had been involved with him, she would have rushed to his side. Heck, she wasn't involved with him, but she had rushed to the hospital as soon as she had seen the news of the explosion at Payne Protection. Of course, she had been trying to find him anyway because the two weeks had already ended with no word from Brenda.

Now she knew why….

"I was there," the woman replied.

Parker's brow furrowed. "You were? Then why didn't you come see me?"

She shrugged, but her thin shoulders were tense. "What do you want to know from the security system?"

He sighed before replying, "I want to know who was here last."

"Sharon Wells," she replied.

Sharon shuddered. She wished she hadn't come along with Parker; she would have rather cut off and given him her finger than see what she had behind the desk.

"Before tonight," Parker specified. "Who was the last one here?"

"Sharon Wells," she repeated. "Two weeks ago."

Parker turned toward her, and now he looked suspicious of her with the intensity of his blue-eyed stare. "You were the last one here?"

"Two weeks ago was when I packed up some of Ethan's stuff and took the cash Brenda gave me to use the past two weeks," she said. "But I couldn't have been the last one to see her…"

"Alive?"

Knowing what that meant, she shook her head. If she had been the last one to see the judge alive, she would have been the one who killed her. If that was what Parker thought, the police would think that, too.

Sirens blared as police cars, lights flashing, sped through the open gate and up to the house. If Sharon was arrested, she had no hope of ever seeing Ethan again.

Panicking, she clutched Parker's arm. "Brenda wasn't alone when I was here last," she said. "Her bodyguard was with her."

And there was no way she could have overpowered that gorilla to hurt Brenda. There was no way she could have hurt Brenda or anyone else. Parker had to believe her. But why would he when she had begun to doubt him?

Even now, she had only this woman's word that she was the last one who had come in or out of the house. She could have erased other names; she could have erased Parker's. Maybe he hadn't really needed her to let him inside the house; maybe he had brought her along only to help him cover his tracks. Maybe he'd been only using her this whole time as a scapegoat.

"Her bodyguard was with the two of you when the judge told you to hide for two weeks and then contact me if you hadn't heard from her?" he asked.

She nodded.

"Who is her bodyguard?"

The woman snorted. "Obviously not someone very good..."

"I—I only know his first name," Sharon said. "Chuck..." Would that be enough information for them to be able to track him down and prove that when Sharon left two weeks ago the judge had still been alive?

She turned toward the door as police officers burst through it—guns drawn. Why were they acting as if the killer was still at the scene? Was he?

Parker and the woman lifted their hands. "We're with Payne Protection," he said, identifying the two of them. "I'm the one who placed the 911 call."

A bald-headed officer nodded at him. "Hey, Park. Are you still protecting the judge?"

Parker shook his head. "If I had been, you wouldn't have been called here." He pointed behind the desk. "We found the judge dead."

"We?" the officer asked.

"Me and Sharon Wells." Finally he pointed to her; maybe he was pointing the finger *at* her. Was he going to try to place the blame on her?

"I'm Sharon Wells," she identified herself. "And I work—*worked,*" she corrected herself, "for Judge Foster."

They began to look at her as Parker had, as if she was a suspect. But she couldn't have hurt her; she couldn't hurt anyone.

But Parker didn't know that about her; he didn't know her. He hadn't even remembered ever meeting her.

And the police didn't know her at all. Since, according to the security system, she was the last one to have seen Brenda alive, then she would be the most likely suspect in her murder.

Would the police be arresting her before they left the

judge's house? And if they arrested her, she didn't have anyone to bail her out. She might never see Ethan again. When she'd brought him to his father, she had known that never seeing him again might be a possibility, but she hadn't realized that she might not see him because she was behind bars for his mother's murder.

Chapter Seven

Parker could not help Sharon now. The police were questioning her the same way that he had—wondering why she was the last person to have seen her employer alive. Only she hadn't been the last person.

And he would prove that for her. But first he had to settle something else. So he hurried across the driveway to chase down the person who had tried sneaking away from the crime scene.

"Why didn't you come see me at the hospital?" Parker asked his sister. Nikki turned away from him again. But he grabbed her shoulder and turned her back.

She squirmed beneath his grasp and ducked away. But before she turned away from him again, he caught the shimmer of tears in her eyes.

"Niks, what's wrong?"

She shrugged. "Nothing..."

"Niks?"

He grabbed her again and didn't let her get away this time as he folded her into a hug. His little sister never cried; she was too tough for that—or at least too determined to prove to her brothers that she was every bit as tough as they were.

"I'm sorry," she said, "so sorry..."

That she hadn't visited him in the hospital?

"It's okay," he assured her. "I didn't mean to make you feel bad." And this was another reason that he had never had a long-term relationship; he wasn't sensitive enough to a woman's feelings.

"I feel bad because it was my fault," she murmured, her voice cracking with emotion.

Thoroughly confused, Parker had to ask, "What was your fault?"

"It was my fault that you nearly got blown up!" she exclaimed.

"You didn't put the bomb in my SUV," he said, unable to follow her logic or understand her guilt. He loved his sister, but he had never understood her as easily as he had his brothers.

"I sent you back out there to change my lunch order," she said, her voice cracking with the tears she fought so hard with furious blinking and sniffling. "If I hadn't, you wouldn't have been hurt…."

"I'm not hurt," he assured her. He ignored the pounding in his head; it had gone down to a dull thud anyway.

"You have a concussion," she said. "You can't even remember the mother of your child…."

She hadn't visited him in the hospital but she had obviously been apprised of everything that had happened there. His family had no secrets from each other.

"Oh, I remember her…." He glanced to where morgue technicians loaded Brenda Foster's body into the back of the coroner's van.

Poor Ethan. He was so young that he wouldn't even remember his mother.

"That's good," Nikki said with a deep breath of relief. "I'm glad your memory is back."

It had never really been gone. He couldn't blame the concussion for not remembering meeting Sharon at the judge's office. With the security at the courthouse, he hadn't had to assess any of them as threats, so he hadn't paid much attention to the people who had already gone through metal detectors and body screeners.

"I'm glad you're here," Parker said even though the information Nikki had recovered from the security system might hurt Sharon more than help her.

He glanced to where she sat in the back of a police car. According to Officer Green, Detective Sharpe had ordered them to bring her down to the police department so that he could personally interrogate her. Sharpe had just recently been promoted—though he hadn't earned it. So he was probably just trying to scare her; he needn't have bothered.

The poor woman had been absolutely terrified when she had found Brenda's body. There was no way she could have killed her. Physically, she wasn't strong enough. Emotionally, she was too sensitive and too empathetic to hurt anyone.

"Did you tell her that I'm your sister?" Nikki asked.

Parker couldn't remember if he had introduced them; he'd been preoccupied with finding the judge's body and with trying to find out who had killed her and how.

If her bodyguard had been there when the judge had sent Sharon and Ethan into hiding, why hadn't he protected Brenda? Why hadn't he even tried?

Parker wouldn't have failed a client like that. He would have died trying to keep her safe. But maybe he *had* failed a client. If he hadn't let Brenda fire him just so they could sleep together, she would still be alive. He wouldn't have let anyone hurt her.

And he wouldn't let anyone hurt Sharon, either.

"When they take her to the police department to give her statement," he told Nikki, "you need to go with her and make sure she stays safe." He didn't want his sister in danger, either, though, so he would call his brother Cooper for backup. After seeing how brutally Brenda had been murdered, Parker was going to heed the judge's warning to trust no one but him. And his family, of course.

"Where are you going?" Nikki asked.

"You tell me," he said. "Find out who this Chuck is who was supposed to be protecting the judge." Logan probably would have known. As the CEO of Payne Protection Agency, he was aware of the other security firms in the area. But those firms were no competition for Payne Protection—obviously.

"There was no Chuck with fingerprint access to the judge's home," Nikki said with a glance at the police car. "Could she have been lying?"

He shook his head. "No." He didn't think Sharon was capable of lying. He never should have doubted her—even for a minute. "Brenda must not have trusted the guy enough to give him access."

"Then why would she have had him protecting her?"

Because she had fired Parker...

Maybe it was his fault that she had been killed....

As Parker had suspected, Logan knew who the Chuck was that worked bodyguard detail. Charles "Chuck" Horowitz.

Parker stood outside the man's apartment; he was supposed to wait for Logan—since his twin had warned that Chuck was more of a mercenary than a bodyguard. His loyalty went to the person who paid him the most. But Parker did not need backup. He preferred that Logan protect his son and their mother. Parker could take care of himself.

Someone had been trying to kill him for two weeks and had not succeeded yet. And that was before Parker had realized the hit was on him. Now that he knew, he was ready.

An outside stairwell led to Chuck Horowitz's second-story combination apartment-office. Brenda had really dropped her standards when she had fired Payne Protection and hired this yahoo.

Glad that he had changed into dark clothes, Parker kept to the shadows as he climbed the stairs. He didn't need to make himself a target for all the people who would take up that hit for the money.

God, he hoped Sharon was safe. His brother Cooper had assured him that nothing would happen to her or Nikki. But while Cooper could protect her on the outside, if she was arrested…

There was nothing Cooper or Parker could do for her but help try to prove her innocence….

The defense lawyer should be able to prove that although Sharon was taller than Brenda, she wasn't strong enough to have so violently broken the woman's neck. Even the coroner should be able to conclude that it would take a very strong man to do something like that.

A twinge of regret and loss struck Parker's heart. One day Ethan might learn, either through the internet or gossip, how brutally his mother had died. Parker knew from experience that people never forgot tragic deaths like his father's. When the day came that Ethan heard about the murder, Parker wanted to be able to tell his son that he had caught and brought his mother's killer to justice.

He reached the narrow landing at the top of the stairs.

But before he could knock on the door, his cell phone vibrated in his pocket. He ignored it and reached for his gun instead. But it continued to vibrate, so he pulled out the cell. And after lowering his voice to a whisper, he answered it. "Damn it, Logan—"

His voice a shout, Logan burst out, "Don't go in there alone!"

"Do you have eyes on me?" He glanced around in the darkness. He wouldn't have put it past his twin to have assigned one of their bodyguards to tail him. It would actually explain why Logan hadn't fought him that hard when Parker had insisted on leaving the safe house.

"I just know you," Logan replied, which really didn't answer Parker's question. "I know that when you're mad you get hotheaded—too hotheaded to wait for backup."

Parker *was* mad. He was mad that someone was trying to kill him. He was mad that someone was trying to kill Sharon. And he was mad that innocent people had died in their places.

"I don't need backup, big brother." Logan would never let him forget that he had entered the world a whole ten minutes before him. "I got this."

"Before he got kicked out of the league some years ago, Chuck Horowitz was a mixed-martial-arts champion. He could kill you with his bare hands."

Parker's guts tightened—not with fear but with certainty. Brenda had been killed with someone's bare hands. An MMA champ would have easily been able to kill her. He'd just thought the bodyguard had failed to protect her. But had he actually murdered her?

Parker tightened his grip on his gun. "A bullet will stop him."

"Wait for me," Logan ordered again. "I'm on my way there."

"I told you to stay with Ethan and Mom." He had no way of knowing if Chuck Horowitz was even in his apartment.

"Candace is protecting them," Logan assured him. Because of her military and police background, Candace was not just their best female bodyguard but also one of their most competent bodyguards overall.

But Parker didn't feel all that reassured. He glanced down toward the dark street. Not even street lamps glowed in this area of town. But yet he caught a glint of something in the enveloping darkness. Either a glint of eyes… or perhaps of metal…like a gun. "You don't have Candace tailing me?"

"Not since you left the judge's mansion."

So he had had the female bodyguard protecting him and Sharon. If only he had known that, he could have left her outside so the poor woman wouldn't have had to see her employer's corpse….

Parker cursed his twin.

"Hey, it was for your protection."

"It would have been better protection if I had known…." Like now. "Is there anyone following me now?"

"I don't know," Logan said. "You've been driving to make sure you wouldn't have a tail…."

Apparently that hadn't worked with Candace. But then, she had a lot of experience as a security expert and, before then, police and military experience. Someone else would have had more trouble following him…unless…

"But *you* know where I am," Parker pointed out. So Logan could have sent someone ahead of him—someone who watched him now from the darkness.

"And I'm almost there," Logan said. "So wait for me..."

What if Chuck Horowitz was the judge's killer? Then he probably hadn't just killed the judge; he had been trying to kill Sharon and Parker, too, which meant he had mistaken Logan and Cooper for Parker more than once already. That wasn't a risk Parker was willing to take. He didn't want Logan taking a bullet meant for him.

So he clicked off his cell and slid it back into his pocket. Then he gripped the gun with both hands and kicked open the door to Chuck Horowitz's office/apartment. Better to take the man by surprise than give him a chance to react or arm himself.

Using the flashlight on the barrel, Parker swung it around the tiny apartment. The place was trashed—really trashed. The couch was overturned and gutted, stuffing strewn across the dirty carpet. Holes had been smashed through the drywall. There had been a hell of a struggle within those walls. If this was what Chuck had done to his own place, maybe Parker should have waited for backup.

But then the beam of his flashlight glanced across a pair of glazed-over eyes. Dead eyes. Parker trained the light on the man tied to the chair behind his desk. From the bloating and the stench, which Parker only noticed now as it overwhelmed the stale odor of cigarette smoke, it was obvious this corpse had been here awhile.

Chuck Horowitz had been tied up and beaten. But Parker noticed something else about him—the scratches on his hands and arms and the side of his face. The mercenary bodyguard hadn't gotten those scratches from whoever had beaten him to death.

He had probably gotten those from the woman he had killed. Brenda had fought him even though she would have known that she couldn't have overpowered him. What she had done was get his DNA under her nails; she had been smart and resourceful as she had provided evidence for police to arrest her killer and for prosecutors to win the trial against him.

But they wouldn't be able to prosecute a dead man. Shortly after he had killed the judge, someone had killed Chuck Horowitz. But before they'd done that, they had torn his place apart looking for something—and they had tortured him to find out where that something was.

What had his killer wanted? Chuck had already killed the judge—undoubtedly for money. Hadn't that been enough?

From the destruction of the apartment and the corpse, Parker suspected that Chuck's killer hadn't found whatever he had been looking for. Maybe that killer thought he or Sharon had whatever they wanted. Did they have something in their possession that they weren't aware they had? Or did they know something that somebody didn't want them knowing? Was that why someone had put out a hit on them, too?

He heard the click of a gun cocking, and then another light, on high beam, flashed in his face—blinding him so that he couldn't see whoever had sneaked into the apartment behind him. But he didn't need to see to know that it wasn't his brother—Logan wouldn't have pulled a gun on him.

And if Logan had sent backup for him, whoever it was wouldn't have pulled a gun on Parker, either. But a hired killer would....

Chapter Eight

Sharon couldn't stop shaking, but she was no longer in shock. She was angry. Parker Payne was supposed to be the one person she could trust, but he had let the police take her down to the station. And he had just disappeared.

How could he desert her like that when she had needed him?

Because he didn't need her. She wasn't the mother of his son. She had no information to lead him to the person who had offered money for his murder. And hers...

She had nothing to offer Parker Payne. So he had offered her nothing. He hadn't even acknowledged her when the police car had driven off with her in the backseat. Of course, he had been preoccupied with the auburn-haired woman.

"I have answered all of your questions," she told the detective who sat across the table from her in the small, windowless interrogation room. "You have no reason to hold me here."

When the officer had questioned her at the hospital, he had used an office with a window. It hadn't been so confining and suffocating.

"You were the last one to see the Honorable Brenda Foster alive," the detective said—again. He had kept repeating it as if that statement alone would force her to confess to something she hadn't done.

And Brenda Foster honorable? Sharon wasn't so sure about that. After working for her awhile and listening to her brag about how she had tricked Parker into fathering her child, Sharon had learned that her idol had had clay feet. Now Brenda had a broken neck. Sharon grimaced as an image of the woman's dead and grotesquely contorted body flashed through her mind.

Her head pounded, too, with stress and exhaustion. Maybe that was part of why she kept shaking. "Her bodyguard was the last person to see her alive," Sharon repeated for the umpteenth time.

"A man whose last name you don't even know," the detective said with the snide little smirk he had been flashing her for the past couple of hours. He was older than her but not by much, so he had apparently made detective young enough that it had gone to his head. "That's quite convenient."

Nothing about this had been convenient for Sharon. Maybe it was the fatigue or the headache, but her tenuous control over the anger she had been feeling snapped. "It's quite convenient that you're forgetting I have rights, Detective Sharpe. Rights that you haven't read me because you have no evidence to put me under arrest."

His smirk widened. "Now I can tell that you've been working for a judge for a while. So then you should know that I can hold you as a material witness—"

"I didn't witness anything." This time. "And I haven't just worked for a judge."

His voice rising with excitement, he leaned across the small, scratched-up metal table. "Oh, you and Judge Foster were more than employee and employer?" He obviously thought he had found a salacious motive for the judge's murder. A lover's quarrel…

Sharon couldn't believe that such an idiot had made detective. He had to know that there was no physical way that she could have broken her boss's neck. So with her temper rising even higher, she pulled out a card she had never played before. "I haven't just worked for a judge," she repeated. "I am the granddaughter of a judge."

He leaned back and lifted a brow. "Really?"

"I am Judge Wells's granddaughter." It wasn't something he had ever freely or happily admitted, but it was an irrefutable fact. Like Judge Foster, police officers had respected Judge Wells for his tough sentences.

The guy leaned forward again and he got *that* look on his face—that look of horror and concern—that told her he knew her story. Even as young as he was, he had heard it. "I'm sorry…."

Not that she was Judge Wells's granddaughter. He was sorry for the rest of it.

"That must have been tough tonight, seeing the judge's corpse…." He shuddered for her.

It had been more than twenty years, but she still occasionally had the nightmares. She had no doubt that she would have one tonight…if she ever slept. She nodded.

"But that doesn't mean that you couldn't have killed her."

She lifted her hands. "I couldn't have. Physically, I couldn't have, and you know that."

He shrugged. "Maybe you used a weapon. Did you really have nothing with you when the officers brought you in?"

She shook her head. "I have no idea what kind of

weapon could have done that to Brenda." Now she shuddered for herself and for her dead employer.

"If that were true, why did you hide your things from the officers at the scene?" he asked.

"What things?" she asked. "I didn't bring anything with me." Thanks to the car explosion, she had nothing left.

The detective sighed, as if frustrated with her. "Miss Wells—"

"You're wasting your time with me when you should be finding Judge Foster's bodyguard," she said. "He was the last one to see her alive—because he was with her when I left her house."

And Chuck had been such a burly man that he wouldn't have needed a weapon to kill Brenda or even a man twice her size. Had Parker gone after him? Was that why he hadn't come to the police department with her?

If he had tracked down Chuck on his own, he could wind up as brutally murdered as Brenda had been. Despite the heat of the stale air in the small room, her blood chilled, and she shivered in reaction.

"You need to find that man right now," she said. Before Parker found him—unless it was already too late.

The detective touched his ear, where he must have been wearing a radio piece. "It's too late," he said, as if he had read her mind.

"What's too late?" she asked, fearfully. Had Parker already found him?

"He's dead."

She gasped as her heart kicked against her ribs. "Who's dead?"

"The bodyguard—Chuck," he said.

Her breath shuddered out in relief. That relief was

short-lived, though, when she realized that just because the bodyguard was dead didn't mean that Parker was alive.

The detective hadn't missed her initial reaction. "That makes you happy? I guess it would since a dead man can't refute your statement."

"Are you going to accuse me of killing him, too?" she wondered aloud. "I don't even know his last name."

"Parker Payne knows it," he said. "He was at the man's apartment when we found his corpse."

That was where Parker had gone. He had tracked down the bodyguard. But what had happened when he'd found him?

She remembered and repeated the detective's choice of word. "Corpse?"

"The coroner thinks Chuck Horowitz died around the same time the judge must have."

So someone had killed them both? She shuddered.

The man leaned forward again, and his eyes narrowed speculatively. "What do you know about Parker Payne, Ms. Wells?"

"That the judge trusted him," she said.

"Do you?" the detective asked.

She had thought she could. But now she wasn't so certain. "If the bodyguard was killed weeks ago, then Parker didn't have anything to do with it."

"Do you know what he was doing weeks ago?"

No. She had been in hiding. If the news was to be believed, though, he had been getting shot at and nearly blown up. "But I think you know."

The detective shrugged. "Payne Protection has definitely been filing a lot of police reports recently."

"Then you know that Parker is in danger." Just like

she was, but if he didn't know about the hit on her, she wasn't going to draw Detective Sharpe's attention to it. Brenda had warned her to trust no one but Parker. Now she was going to trust no one—not even Parker.

"Or maybe he *is* the danger. I thought you just needed to watch out for him because he's a playboy, but maybe you need to watch out for him because he's a killer," the detective warned her.

She shook her head. "He's not shooting at himself or trying to blow himself up."

"But he could have killed the judge," the detective persisted. "He could have also killed the bodyguard."

"And gone back tonight?" she asked. "Why?"

Detective Sharpe shrugged again. "Your grandfather never told you about the criminals who returned to the scenes of their crimes?"

"Parker Payne is no criminal." Her instinctive defense of him laid to rest those doubts she'd kept having about him. While her mind found reasons why she shouldn't trust him, her gut trusted him instinctively. Her heart trusted him.

The detective cocked his head as if considering the veracity of her statement; he obviously didn't know and respect Parker like the older officer who had spoken with her at the hospital or the bald-headed officer at the judge's house.

"I would have agreed with you," Sharpe admitted, "but he has recently started associating with some known criminals."

She shrugged now. She had no idea with whom Parker associated. "I wouldn't know—"

"The Kozminskis," he said, as if she had asked. "They were at the hospital earlier when the bomb went off in the parking lot. They were with their new brother-in-law—Logan Payne."

They must have been the blond men with the light-colored eyes who had found out that someone had put out a hit on her as well as Parker.

"The Kozminskis have long criminal records," Detective Sharpe continued, "starting with stints in juvie for theft and murder…."

"I don't know the Kozminskis." But if they were any part of the reason for her interrogation, she didn't like them very much. "I have nothing to do with any of this. Not only am I physically incapable of doing—" an involuntary shudder struck her with the memory of Brenda's corpse "—what was done to the judge, but I have no motive to hurt her. Now that she's dead I have no job."

No mentor to help her pass the bar. Not that Brenda had been much help on Sharon's previous attempts. She had even suggested that Sharon give up on law and continue as Ethan's nanny. Now she wouldn't even be able to do that—and that was the far greater loss to Sharon.

The detective snorted. "You have the biggest motive, Ms. Wells."

"Unemployment?" she scoffed.

"Inheritance."

The detective had obviously lost it. "What inheritance?" The judge hadn't even paid her that well.

"When the judge's murder was reported on television, her lawyer contacted us about her child. He thought the child would be with you…."

"He—he's with…friends." Given the detective's opinion of the Paynes and the Kozminskis, she didn't dare be more specific, or else he might send a police car to pick up Ethan, too.

"The judge's will made you the guardian of her son and the trustee of the estate he'll inherit from her—a sizable estate from which you'll draw a sizable salary for his care." His smirk was back. "That gives you a very big motive for her murder."

"I am Judge Wells's granddaughter," she reminded the dim-witted detective. "I don't need money." And maybe that was why Brenda hadn't paid her very much. The judge had known what Sharon had inherited when her grandparents had passed away a few years ago—a lot of money. But they had never given Sharon what she had really wanted from them: their love.

"I would never kill anyone…."

"Not even for that little boy?" he asked. "The judge must have really trusted you with him to appoint you as his guardian in her will."

Sharon had lied to the detective…because Ethan was the one person for whom she would kill. She would do anything to protect that little boy.

She shrugged. "I never really knew what Judge Foster was thinking or what she was involved in. You will need to investigate *her* life to find out who killed her. Not mine." Because Sharon had never really had much of a life. She had studied and she had worked. "So unless you're going to press charges, I'm leaving, Detective."

She stood up and walked to the door. She tried to turn the knob, but it was locked in place. He had locked her inside the interrogation room, the small, windowless room. All those memories that had already rushed over her once that evening rushed back again, overwhelming her.

Her legs weakened, and her shaking body dropped to the floor. She briefly registered the hardness of the concrete beneath her before she passed out.

PARKER'S HEART BEAT a frantic pace as he watched the paramedics wheel Sharon's unconscious body into the hospital, where he had been pacing the emergency room while he waited for her arrival. "You were supposed to protect her!" he yelled at his sister as soon as she ran in behind the paramedics.

As Cooper followed Nikki inside, he shook his head. "Back off. She couldn't go into the interrogation room with her."

"She was hurt in the interrogation room?" he asked. "Who the hell was interrogating her?"

"Sharpe," Nikki reminded him.

Parker's temper flared with frustration with himself and with the detective. That little weasel wouldn't have made detective if his mother wasn't the chief's little sister. "I'll kill him."

The jerk already thought Parker was a killer. He had actually had a police officer following him from the judge's house to the bodyguard's apartment. Parker had nearly shot the damn kid who'd been too scared at Chuck Horowitz's crime scene to identify himself as a police officer. If not for Logan showing up behind the kid…

"Don't go making any threats," Logan advised as he showed up behind Parker now.

"But what the hell did he do to her?"

Nikki and Cooper both shrugged. His younger brother replied, "He had her in the interrogation room for a long time."

"And she was already in shock from the crime scene," Nikki added, her dark eyes flashing with frustration. "She should have gone from the judge's house to the hospital, not to the police station."

Detective Sharpe stepped through the doors behind

Nikki and Cooper. But before Parker could reach for his scrawny little neck, Logan pulled him back. "No threats. Calm down," his older brother advised. "Or he will have the authority to arrest you this time."

"Let him," Parker growled. Then he whirled on Sharpe. "What the hell did you do to her?"

The man's eyes widened. "What did *I* do? It's what *you* did—bringing *Sharon Wells* to a murder scene!"

"I didn't know it was a murder scene," he said. "Any more than I knew that there was a murder scene at Chuck Horowitz's house."

The man nodded with a patronizing smile pasted on his pallid face. "That's what all the criminals say…."

"Okay, maybe you should hit him," Logan remarked. "You're way out of line here, Sharpe."

Parker didn't care what the jerk said about him. He cared about Sharon. "What did you mean about Sharon? What do you know about her?"

"You don't know who she is?" Sharpe asked smugly.

Parker really wanted to hit him. "Just tell me what you know…" He bit off the insult he wanted to add; it wouldn't get him anywhere when the man thought so highly of himself. "…about Sharon."

"She's Judge Wells's granddaughter…."

Judge Wells? The name sounded vaguely familiar. Maybe Parker had testified before him in a drug-arrest case back in the days when he'd worked undercover vice for River City P.D. He shrugged. "I don't remember much about him."

"Guess you only pay attention to the female judges."

He really, really wanted to hit him now, but he restrained himself. "How old is this Judge Wells?" After all, he was her *grandfather.*

"He's dead."

"Then how would I know the guy?"

"Ooooh." The word slipped out of Nikki with a sudden nod of understanding.

"Your sister knows," Sharpe said, "and she's younger than you are."

He turned toward Nikki; he would rather hear it from her than the defective detective anyway. "What do you know, Niks?"

Nikki shuddered. "It was a tragic story…."

"Oh," Logan said. "I remember…."

"Where was I?" Parker wondered.

"We were kids when it happened," Logan said. "It's just that people seemed to bring it up every time they talked about the judge…."

Like people had brought up their father's murder every time they talked about any other Payne. Yeah, they never forgot tragic deaths.

"Who died?" Parker asked.

"Sharon's mother," Nikki said. "She was really young. She was just a teenager when she had Sharon. The story goes that the judge and his wife didn't approve, so she ran away from home. She was working nights at a gas station—" her forehead creased as she searched her memory "—or a convenience store when she was murdered."

"That's awful," Parker said. Like Ethan, Sharon had also lost her mother when she was young. She would be able to identify with the little boy even more than she already seemed to.

Nikki shuddered again. "What was worse is that the girl couldn't afford a babysitter, so she brought Sharon to work with her. She was there when her mother was murdered."

"How old was she?" Old enough to remember?

"I think three or four," Nikki said. "When customers came in, her mother would have her crawl into a cupboard behind the counter. The killer didn't know she was there or she probably would have been killed, too."

Horror gripped Parker. "Do you think she saw what happened?"

"She picked the killer out of a line-up." Logan chimed in with the detail that he, as a former detective, would of course remember best.

"At three or four years old?" he asked in disbelief. He knew that young witnesses weren't always the most reliable. But then, the face of her mother's killer was probably one Sharon would never forget—even more than twenty years later. "Did she testify?"

"It didn't go to trial," Logan said. "The killer didn't know there was a witness, so he confessed."

At least she had been spared a trial. But the horror she must have witnessed…and finding Brenda murdered so violently had probably brought back all the old nightmares. He had to talk to her doctor. But would her doctor talk to him?

Parker was nobody to her. He wasn't family. He wasn't even her friend or he wouldn't have left her alone to deal with the police. But he hadn't known….

He'd had no idea how upset she must have been. He couldn't keep his anger to himself, though, so he reached out for Sharpe. But Logan dragged him back. "You know all this about her and you still interrogated her in some little room? You sadistic blowhard! You have to know that she couldn't have hurt her employer."

"Maybe she wasn't strong enough to have broken the judge's neck," the detective admitted. "But we know that she was the last one to go past the security system. We don't know if she was alone."

"She wasn't," Parker said. "The bodyguard was with Brenda."

"I meant Ms. Wells," he said. "She may have brought someone with her—someone who killed the judge for her."

He was an even bigger idiot than Parker had thought. "Really? So she willingly put herself through witnessing another murder? That's ridiculous."

"It really is," Logan added. "Have you ever even cleared a case, Sharpe?"

Finally color flushed the man's pasty face, giving Logan his answer.

"She has no motive, either," Parker pointed out.

"The judge made her trustee of the estate with a generous income."

Nikki laughed. "She's Judge Wells's granddaughter. I hardly think she needs money."

The color deepened in Sharpe's face. "But she doesn't just get money out of the deal. She gets the kid, too."

"What?" Parker asked.

"Brenda Foster's will awards Sharon Wells custody of the kid."

"But the kid has a father," Parker pointed out. He was Ethan's father. But he wasn't about to announce that in front of Sharpe and provide the man with his own motive for killing Brenda.

Sharpe shook his head. "Birth certificate states father unknown. She probably used a sperm donor."

Now Parker's face was the one that flushed with embarrassment. He had been a sperm donor—but an unwitting one. He had even insisted on using a condom, but Brenda must have compromised it somehow.

"But if someone can prove he's the boy's father," Parker persisted, "as the sole parent, he would become the boy's guardian."

Sharpe shrugged. "It would probably go to court. He'd have to fight for custody. I doubt he would have killed the judge because it probably just complicates his life."

So Parker was off the hook for murder. And fatherhood?

But he wanted his son. He wanted to fight, but he didn't want to fight a woman who had already been through too much in her life. Could Sharon even handle a fight?

Hell, she couldn't handle any more attempts on her life. Parker would deal with the custody issue after he'd dealt with whoever wanted him and Sharon dead.

Chapter Nine

If someone can prove he's the boy's father...

The words she had heard as she'd walked out to join the others in the waiting room still rang in Sharon's ears now, as she stared down at the sleeping baby.

Why had they been waiting for her? She was scarcely more than a stranger to them. But when they had turned toward her, she'd seen it on all of their faces—that overly solicitous concern that told her they knew. They knew what had happened to her mother. And they thought that witnessing it had made Sharon fragile.

Weak.

And passing out in the interrogation room had only proved their opinion of her. Would Parker use that against her in court when he fought her for custody of his child?

"Didn't he even wake up?" Sharon asked the boy's grandmother. She had been gone so long, away from the baby for far longer than she had wanted to be away.

"He woke up," Mrs. Payne said with a sigh. "And he cried most of the time you were gone. He only fell back to sleep a short while ago."

So he had cried for hours without her?

When Parker exercised his parental rights, she would be away from Ethan for far longer than a few hours. She would be cut out of the rest of his life. And he wouldn't remember her any more than he was likely to remember his dead mother.

Tears stung her eyes, but she blinked them back. Too many of the Paynes already thought she was weak.

But Mrs. Payne must have caught her action because she rubbed her back, as she probably had the crying baby's to soothe him to sleep. "While he's sleeping, you should get some rest. You must be exhausted."

She had been exhausted a couple of sleepless nights ago. She was beyond exhausted now. But she worried that if she slept, she wouldn't see Ethan again. "I—I just want to watch him sleep...."

To assure herself that he was all right, that he wasn't gone like his mother, like the bodyguard, like all those people who had died for no reason that she could fathom...

She and Parker had come no closer to learning why someone wanted them dead; they had only found more dead. The tears threatened again. She blinked harder but one slipped through her lashes and rolled down her cheek to drop onto the sleeping baby. Her breath caught, but he only sighed.

Next to her, Mrs. Payne had tensed, but she relaxed with the child. "It's like he knows you're here. He recognizes his mother's presence."

But Sharon wasn't his mother. And she was probably only his guardian for now...until a judge decided the biological father's rights overruled hers.

She shook her head. "No, I—I'm not..."

Why hadn't Parker told his family right away? He'd been upset with her for letting him believe she was the baby's mother. Why had he let his family believe it even after he'd learned the truth?

"Judge Foster was Ethan's mother," Sharon said. "And I worked for her—first as her law clerk and then as her nanny." Brenda had kept telling her that she didn't have the aptitude to be a lawyer, and Sharon's failed attempts at passing the bar supported that supposition.

All those years she had spent in school and studying...

And she'd found what she loved by default. She had found Ethan because Brenda hadn't been able to keep any other nanny working for her.

"You love him like he's yours," Mrs. Payne observed. "And he loves and relies on you like you're his mother."

She nodded. "I do love him—very much." And if she hadn't been afraid that she wouldn't be able to keep him safe on her own, she might not have brought him to Parker. But she wasn't equipped to protect him from fires and bombs.... Eventually he would have been hurt just from being around her. Maybe the best thing for the boy would be for her to turn down the guardianship and let the Paynes have him.

"Are you going to fight me?" Parker asked.

She was so tired that she hadn't even heard him climb the stairs to the top-floor master bedroom, where he'd set up that portable crib what seemed like so long ago.

"Fight you?" Mrs. Payne asked. Her brow furrowed as she turned toward her son, clearly puzzled.

It wasn't her place to tell the woman what her son had not, but Sharon found herself explaining, "Judge Foster gave me guardianship of Ethan in her will."

She was sorry that the woman was dead, but she still resented how she had treated her son—more like a possession than a person. But then, Brenda Foster had been too busy to get to know the little boy, to appreciate how smart and affectionate he was.

Mrs. Payne continued to stare at her son. "Then why would *she* fight *you?*"

He furrowed his brow now, obviously as confused as she had been with him. "Because there is no way that I am going to give up my son."

Pain struck Sharon's heart. "So because I'm not his blood relative, you would cut me out of his life?" Then anger surged within her and the heat of it dried up her tears. "I've been with him pretty much every day since he was born, and you expect me to just give him up? To just walk away?"

That was what her grandparents had expected her mother to do—to give up her baby to strangers. To just give her up and walk away and forget all about her.

But maybe they'd been right. Maybe if her mother had, she would still be alive—since she would have been in college and not working at a convenience store in a bad area of the city.

"Nobody's asking you to do that," Mrs. Payne said.

Sharon stared at Parker; he wasn't asking. But it was what he expected.

"A judge might," Parker said.

"A judge might not care that he has your DNA," Sharon replied. "You didn't even know about him until I brought him to you."

"You're probably regretting that now," he remarked, his blue eyes glittering with sarcasm and resentment. He had every right to be angry that she had been awarded guardianship over him—but she was not the one he should be angry with.

She had actually regretted not telling him earlier. She'd thought the judge was wrong to keep him from his child. But then she remembered her excuse for doing that. "According to Brenda, you never wanted to be a father."

"That's why she tricked me."

There were other reasons why Brenda had admitted that she had chosen Parker as the father of her baby: because he was smart and handsome and protective and had the kind of charisma that drew everyone to him. But Sharon didn't want to tell him that and add to his argument for custody.

"You have said before—a lot—that you never wanted to be a father," Mrs. Payne agreed.

Parker sucked in a breath. "Mom, whose side are you on?"

She pointed toward the sleeping baby. "I'm on my grandson's side. I don't want him to have to give up either one of you. And if you take each other to court, you might both lose him."

Sharon sucked in the breath now. That hadn't occurred to her.

"If you both prove the other unworthy of parenthood, the judge might put Ethan into the foster-care system," Mrs. Payne pointed out. "Doesn't a judge still have to approve this guardianship?"

There had been so much going on with the attacks and the murders that Sharon hadn't considered that there was more to the process than just Brenda granting her guardianship of Ethan.

What if a judge didn't approve? Given her history as a woman with a traumatic past, she might not be considered emotionally stable enough to be a guardian.

"And just because you're his father doesn't mean you'll automatically get him," Mrs. Payne continued. "You've never had any interest in children or in being a father—"

"That was before I knew that I am a father," Parker replied defensively.

Sharon reached out and grasped Parker's arm; his muscles tensed beneath her touch. She was tense, too. "We can't lose him to the system."

Too many kids got lost in the system. Her grandfather had definitely made certain she was aware of what could have happened to her if he and her grandmother hadn't been gracious enough to take custody of her after her mother's murder.

Parker narrowed his eyes and studied his mother. "So you must have a plan for your grandson since you have a plan for everyone. What do you propose we do?"

"Propose," Mrs. Payne said. "Marry her."

Sharon must have fallen asleep; she had to be dreaming. Because there was no way that anyone would have suggested that she—shy, quiet Sharon Wells—marry a devastatingly handsome playboy like Parker Payne. But it didn't matter whether or not it was a dream because it would never become reality. Parker Payne would never ask her to marry him.

By the time he had gotten rid of everyone else, Sharon had fallen asleep in the middle of the king-sized bed in the master suite. And he found himself standing over her, watching her sleep.

She was exhausted. That was the excuse she had given for passing out during her interrogation, the reason she had given for checking herself out of the emergency room before the doctor had even seen her. The dark circles beneath her eyes proved her weariness.

But the way she murmured and twitched in her sleep betrayed her stress. And her fear. Finding the judge dead must have brought all those horrible memories rushing back to her.

He wanted to gather her into his arms and hold her close—to protect her. Maybe his mother was right. Maybe he should marry her. Not just so they would have a better chance at keeping Ethan but also so Parker could protect her.

He was no closer to finding out who wanted them dead. Certainly it involved the judge, but how had Brenda dragged him and Sharon into whatever mess she'd created?

He had lost touch with Brenda—probably shortly after she'd conceived Ethan. He needed to delve into her life more and find out what she'd been up to, and nobody knew her life better than Sharon did.

That was probably why Sharon was in danger. She had to know something that she wasn't even aware that she knew. And that something had put her life at risk.

Brenda had put her life at risk.

He had to protect Sharon. He leaned down and reached out for her, skimming his fingertips across her cheek. Her skin was so smooth, so silky. She was young—probably even younger than he'd realized when he had first seen her with her hair in a tight knot. Her severe suit had also made her look older. But now with the jacket discarded on the floor and her blouse all rumpled, she looked like a teenager who had dressed up in her mother's clothes for an interview.

But after witnessing what she had at such a young age, had she ever really had a normal life? She must have grown up so fast. By picking her mother's killer out of a line-up, she had been the one to bring him to justice. To get justice for her mother…

He wanted to get justice for Ethan—for *his* mother. But he also wanted to keep safe the woman whom Ethan probably saw as his mother, the woman who had actually been taking care of him. Sharon.

Marrying her wouldn't be enough to keep her safe, though. He had to find out who was after them before they wound up like Brenda and her bodyguard....

Dead.

A cry broke the eerie silence of the penthouse. It hadn't come from the baby, though. It had slipped through the parted lips of the woman. A whimper full of pain and fear followed it.

It pierced his heart. He cupped her cheek in his palm. "Sharon..."

She was exhausted, but he would rather wake her up than leave her in such a state.

"Sharon..."

Her thick lashes fluttered as if she struggled to wake. Or maybe it was the dream—the nightmare—that she struggled to escape. Finally her eyes—those enormous light brown eyes—opened, and she stared up at him.

But the fear didn't leave her face. It was as if it increased, as if she'd become more afraid. Was she afraid of him? Because of the custody thing or because of the suspicions that he'd seen on her expressive face back at Brenda's house?

She must have wondered if he had killed her boss. She might even wonder if he'd killed the bodyguard, too.

But then she reached out, as if trying to hold on to him—as if seeking his protection. And he heard it, too. The footsteps on the stairs. She knew he had gotten rid of everyone, that he had told them not to come back until he called for them.

Logan was the boss—as he always pointed out—but even he respected that this time Parker was giving the orders. The only one who might have disregarded his wishes was his mother, but she'd wanted to give them time alone—to think about her suggestion of marrying.

And while Logan might have thought about crossing Parker, he wouldn't disobey their mother. That was how *he* had wound up married.

His mother was so convinced that she was right that she was sure he would realize it, too, if she gave him enough time. So she wouldn't have let anyone disturb him.

He reached for his gun. But he didn't want any more dead bodies and not just because Sharon didn't need to see another one.

But because dead bodies meant dead ends.

If he killed whoever was coming after him and Sharon, he wouldn't be able to find out who had sent that person. He needed his would-be assassin capable of talking.

But if he didn't use the gun, he risked the person getting away or taking him down first. That meant he was putting Sharon and Ethan in danger.

He reached for the gun again, but then he pressed it into her hands. And he leaned close to whisper in her ear. "If it looks like he's getting the best of me, pull the trigger. I took the safety off…."

She gasped in protest of taking the gun. But he hadn't given her a choice.

He turned toward the stairwell. But he couldn't risk the intruder reaching the top and maybe firing wild shots around the room, taking them both out. So he vaulted over the railing and rushed down the steps.

Chapter Ten

The gun was heavy and cold in her hands. Sharon wanted to slide the safety back on and put it aside. But curses and grunts and groans emanated from the stairwell while Parker struggled with whoever had broken into the condo.

And then Ethan awoke with a startled cry, which quickly became screams of utter terror as the loud fighting in the stairwell continued.

"Shhh, sweetheart…I'm here," she assured him. "You're safe."

But was she lying to him?

She rose carefully from the bed, the gun grasped in her trembling hands. Keeping the barrel pointed away from the crib, she walked toward it and the screaming baby. "Shhh…"

He kicked his feet and flailed his arms, reaching for her. And she wanted to reach for him. But if she put down the gun…

If Parker needed her…

"You're okay, little man," she told the baby. But she wasn't so sure about his daddy. So she moved back toward the stairwell and peered over the side, over the barrel of the gun she held. The men were a tangle of arms and legs. She couldn't make out who was who.

But she did see the glint of metal in the beam of sunshine pouring through the skylights above the stairwell. While Parker had handed her his weapon, the intruder had brought one of his own.

A gun?

A knife?

She couldn't tell. Yet…

But if Parker needed her to defend him, she would shoot. She would not let Ethan lose his mother and his father….

FEAR AND REGRET chilled his blood as Parker stared down the barrel of a gun. He should not have given his weapon to Sharon—especially since she was now pointing his Glock at him.

"I come here to warn you and this is how you thank me," Garek Kozminski grumbled. "You break my neck on the damn stairs…."

Sharon gasped, no doubt as the memory of Brenda's corpse flashed through her mind as it just had his. The gun shook in her trembling hands. Not only was she scared, but the weapon was probably too heavy for her given how exhausted she was.

Why had he taken off the safety?

He elbowed Garek, who cursed in protest. "Show some sensitivity, man…."

"Show some appreciation," he retorted. "I've got important news."

When Parker had first realized that the man he'd attacked on the stairs was Logan's brother-in-law, he had been relieved. But now it occurred to him that Garek Kozminski wasn't someone he should trust. The Payne family tradition was law enforcement or protection; the

Kozminski family tradition was jewelry thieving. But that wasn't the only crime Garek had committed; he had also killed.

And if he'd done it once…

"Why didn't you go to Logan with your important news?" he wondered.

"I thought you were running this show," Garek replied. "That's what you said at the hospital."

It was….

"But how did you find *me?*"

Garek grunted and shoved, trying to lever Parker off him. But Parker wasn't ready yet to let the man up. He wanted to stay between him and Sharon. Although maybe that wasn't the safest place for him given that Sharon's grasp on the loaded gun was so shaky….

"I've been tailing you," Garek admitted.

"How?" He had been careful to avoid any tails or so he'd thought. But the rookie cop had followed him and apparently so had a criminal….

Garek shrugged. "Don't get all bent out of shape like your brother did when I tailed him. You guys are good at losing tails, but I'm better at—"

"Stalking?"

"I am not a stalker," he said, and now he was the one with wounded pride.

"Then why are you holding a knife?" Sharon asked, her voice sharp with suspicion.

As Garek flashed the blade in question, Sharon steadied the barrel of the gun. She was ready to shoot. Despite everything she had been through and her exhaustion, she was prepared to protect him—better than he had been protecting her.

"I cannot say exactly what this is," Garek began, "since

I am not allowed to possess any tools for breaking and entering. But hypothetically speaking, this looks more like a lock pick than a knife…." He glanced at it as if considering how much damage he could do with it. "It probably couldn't cause a wound much deeper than a paper cut."

Parker could have called him on that lie since it had sliced through his shirt and grazed his skin. But then he was worried that Sharon might shoot. Hell, maybe he should let her.

"I don't understand why you tailed me here and broke in," he said. And he had some big concerns about the man's motives. "Logan would have preferred you'd gone through him."

"I don't want Logan putting himself and my sister in the line of fire," Garek said. And that reply made more sense than him wanting to tell Parker directly. "She was nearly killed because she was with him when he was mistaken for you. My sister's already been through too much…."

And her brother had blamed Logan for that. Now he knew that Parker was really the one to blame. But then maybe he had reasoned that if he killed Parker, people would stop trying to kill his twin.

"Sharon has already been through too much, too," Parker said. And he glanced up again, but she—and the gun barrel—were both gone. She must have determined that Garek was no threat. Or she had decided that Ethan needed her more than Parker did because the baby's cries had subsided. "Don't hurt her."

"You think I came here to hurt you?" Garek asked, his voice gruff with more than wounded pride. "I came here to warn you, to help you…" He shoved off Parker and struggled to his feet, groaning as his body shifted.

Parker had hurt him, but probably more emotionally than physically. Maybe since their siblings had married, Kozminski had begun to feel as if they were family. Parker had begun to feel that way, too, until he had suddenly gained an instant family of his own with Ethan and…Sharon. He wasn't sure what she was, but before he had even known that the baby was his, he had witnessed that she and the boy were as connected as if they were mother and son.

His mother was right. *Damn her...*

"I'm sorry," Parker said. "I just have to be careful…."

"You have to be more careful now," Garek advised.

"Why? What have you learned?" What information did he have that was so important that he'd broken into the condo to share it?

"The reward for your murders has been doubled," Garek said. "And it was already a generous amount of money for a hit." He shook his head, as if he was dumbfounded. "Now it's an *obscene* amount of money."

Parker cursed.

And Sharon appeared at the top of the stairwell. Those enormous eyes wide with concern, she stared down at him. Apparently she had heard only his curses, not what Garek had said. "What's going on?"

He wished he knew. Why was someone so determined that he and Sharon die?

"You should tell her," Garek advised.

Parker wasn't sure she could handle knowing how badly someone wanted her dead. But then he remembered how her grip had steadied on the gun and how she had been ready to shoot to protect him.

"Tell me what?" she asked, and as she stepped closer

to the stairs, he noticed the baby in her arms. Ethan clung to her, his little fingers tangled in her hair.

While Parker was his father, *she* was the boy's security. Ethan couldn't lose her. The greatest thing Parker could do as the boy's father was to make sure he kept this woman safe. "Whoever wants us dead upped the ante."

He wasn't sure she would understand, but she nodded and sucked in an audibly shaky breath. And then with the boy balanced on one of her lean hips, she pulled the gun out with the hand on her other side. The barrel was pointed straight and steady down the stairwell.

Garek laughed. "So *she's* going to shoot you to collect?"

"I have money," Sharon said. "I'll pay you to leave us alone."

Garek tensed as he realized what she thought, that she had the same suspicion that Parker had briefly entertained. "I have never met two more ungrateful people," he murmured. "I come here to warn you and you both think that I came here to collect on the damn rewards."

"I'm sorry," she said. "But you're a Kozminski, right?"

He hesitated but nodded.

"Detective Sharpe warned me about you."

Garek sighed. "Of course he did."

"He warned me about Parker, too."

Garek laughed. "I knew the guy was an idiot. But you have nothing to fear from any one of the Paynes—they're all about law and order." But he notably didn't make that claim for himself. "You're safer with this guy than you would be with anybody else—probably even with the police right now."

Parker flinched as he remembered how the greed of a certain police officer had cost both him and Garek their fathers. Parker's dad had died and Garek's dad had gone to prison for killing him even though another man had pulled the trigger. Parker hadn't had time to deal yet with finding out how his father's partner had betrayed him before he'd found out that someone was trying to kill him.

And then he had found out he was a father....

No wonder his head was pounding now. It wasn't just because of the concussion or exhaustion...

He was overwhelmed.

No doubt so was Sharon. So many people had been telling her so many things. Was it any wonder that she might struggle over what to believe and whom to trust?

She said, "Detective Sharpe warned me that Parker's a playboy."

Garek laughed harder—so hard that the baby laughed with him. "Maybe Sharpe's not as big an idiot as I thought...."

"He's an idiot," Parker insisted to Sharon. Then he turned back to Garek. "And *you* have no room to talk in the playboy department."

He laughed again. "I'm not denying that...."

Parker couldn't deny his reputation, either. He had vowed to never marry, to never have children. But he'd had reasons. He had actually wanted to spare someone mourning him the way he and his mother and siblings had mourned the loss of their father. And even before the hit had gone out on him, his life had often been in jeopardy. As an undercover cop, he'd put his life on the line with every dangerous assignment. And when he protected someone, he again placed himself between that person and potential danger.

"Thanks for breaking and entering," Parker said, "to give us the heads-up."

Garek shrugged and winced. "Don't mention it. I'd stay to help protect you and all, but I'm a lousy shot. And I should probably stop by the emergency room and have them x-ray my ribs."

"Sorry about that," Parker said with a carefully light slap on Garek's shoulder.

"I would have called…"

But Parker had pulled the battery out of his phone so no one would have been able to hack the GPS and find out where he was. He pulled another phone from his pocket. "I replaced my cell with this one. It's an untrace-able track phone." He gave the number to Garek. "Now you can call next time…."

"Let's hope there isn't a next time. You don't want the reward getting tripled." He grinned. "Or I might be tempted to collect." Then he turned and headed down the stairs to the basement garage.

Parker wasn't so sure that Kozminski was kidding. If double an already generous reward was obscene, then triple would probably prove irresistible.

After the door clicked behind Garek, Parker made sure it was locked and the alarm was engaged. Then he headed up the stairs to where Sharon waited for him. Instead of the gun, she held a bottle, which Ethan was eagerly sucking down. She arched her neck to indicate where she had left his weapon sitting on the nightstand next to the rumpled king-sized bed.

He only noticed how delicate her neck looked; how slender she was. Vulnerable. And beautiful…even as ex-hausted as she was.

She hadn't had much sleep, and it showed in the dark circles beneath her enormous eyes. After what they had just learned from Garek, she probably wouldn't be able to go back to sleep even if Ethan did.

"I'm sorry about that," he said.

She skeptically arched a brow. "Sorry that he made you tell me?"

"Yes," he admitted.

"Why?" she asked, and she bristled with pride. "Do you think I'm too weak or fragile to know what's going on? That the reward for our murders has been increased?"

He glanced again to where she'd put the gun. "You handled that pretty well."

Her mouth curved into a slight smile. "Don't patronize me. I could barely hold on to it. But that wasn't because I'm weak or fragile. It's because I don't like guns."

Probably with good reason. Had her mother been shot? Or worse…

And at a young, impressionable age, Sharon had seen that and survived. "I don't think you're weak or fragile," he assured her.

She narrowed her eyes and stared at him suspiciously. "Are you still patronizing me?"

"No," he said. "I know how strong you have to be when you lose a parent."

She gasped. "Oh, that's right…." Her face flushed a bright red with embarrassment. "I'm sorry…."

"You know about my dad?" he asked.

"Brenda told me that he died when you were a teenager," she said. "And then I saw on the news that it was just discovered that another man killed him than the one who'd been in prison for his murder."

"Garek's dad was the man in prison for his murder," he said, "until he died there."

Her brows lifted in surprise. "And his sister is married to your brother?"

Parker laughed. "They used to hate each other—or so they claimed. But Stacy always knew it wasn't her dad who had killed ours." A twinge of pain struck his chest over the betrayal that had led to his dad's death. "She was right. It wound up being another officer—his partner."

She nodded. "Brenda told me not to trust the police."

"I can't argue with her now," he said. "I'd like to say they can't be bought. But some of them can be more greedy than honorable." He wondered about Sharpe and that kid that Sharpe had sent to follow him. Why hadn't he identified himself as an officer when he'd pulled the gun on Parker? What might have happened if Logan hadn't shown up?

"And the reward to kill us is a lot of money?" she asked nervously.

He wasn't going to patronize her with a lie, so he answered honestly. "An obscene amount, according to Garek."

Her arm tightened around Ethan protectively, and she glanced around the condo as if looking for more intruders. He glanced around, too, just in case....

Since Garek had so easily followed him and broken in, someone else could, too. They really weren't safe anywhere. And because they were in danger, so was his son. And if something happened to either one of them or both, what would become of Ethan?

Would Parker's mother be able to get custody or would the baby go straight into the foster-care system? He had to protect his son and Sharon.

Her skin had grown pale, her eyes wide and dark with

fear. Her voice even trembled a bit when she asked, "What do we do now?"

Ignoring the twinge of panic striking his bachelor heart, he replied, "We get married."

Chapter Eleven

Sharon stared at herself in the oval mirror—unable to believe that was actually her reflection staring back at her. How was that her in the lacy, strapless white dress and veil? She had pulled back the veil so that she could see, so that the image would be clear.

But nothing was clear to her. Why did someone so desperately want both her and Parker dead? With the reward for their murders doubled, it was probably only a matter of time before one of the attempts was successful.

Her stomach pitched. She couldn't remember the last time she had eaten. She wasn't worried about marrying the notorious playboy Payne, either. She wasn't about to give him her heart. The only thing she really had to lose was Ethan. And her life.

"I've seen a lot of brides in this room, but I have never seen one look as scared as you do," a female voice remarked. "But then, you're the one marrying Parker."

Sharon turned to see the young auburn-haired woman who had been at Brenda's house and at the police station and at the hospital with her. The young woman had been nearly everywhere that Sharon had, so maybe she should have expected her to show up here. But still, she gasped in surprise.

And the woman wasn't alone; she had brought an enormous dog with her. As it sniffed around the bride's room, Sharon realized it was Cujo—the K9 dog that Parker had previously and wistfully mentioned. He had brought the dog to the wedding to sniff out any bombs. But the German shepherd was disinterested in everything in the room—even Sharon.

"I didn't mean to scare you more," the woman said.

Sharon remembered her solicitous look from the hospital; the woman obviously knew about her tragic past. And pitied her. "I'm fine," she said. "How about you?"

Was she upset that Parker was marrying another woman?

The young woman sighed before replying, "No. With all my brothers married, Mom's going to have no one left to manipulate into marriage but me."

"Brothers?"

She snorted in disgust. "Parker still hasn't told you that I'm his sister?" She thrust her hand between them. "I'm Nikki Payne."

Sharon clasped the proffered hand and firmly shook it. "I'm glad to meet you." Finally…

And she felt like a fool for that fleeting jealousy she had felt—and to which she'd had no right. She and Parker were nothing to each other even though they were about to become husband and wife.

"He should have introduced us at the judge's house," Nikki said. "But I was still a mess from him nearly getting blown up earlier."

It hadn't occurred to Sharon until now how the attempts on his life must have been affecting his family. "And here *I* thought I was the mess…"

"You were," Nikki said with the Payne directness. But

then she laughed. Was she only kidding? "But you had every right. Parker didn't even let me see the body, so it must have been bad." She slapped her hand over her own mouth. "God, I'm so crass."

"You're honest and straightforward," Sharon said. "I appreciate that—even though I haven't been that straightforward myself."

Nikki chuckled again. "You messed with Parker—letting him think you'd had his kid and that he didn't even remember you."

Was his sister angry about that? Sharon opened her mouth to apologize.

But Nikki continued, "That's great. For all the hearts he's broken, he deserved that!"

Sharon shook her head. "He didn't deserve to be kept in the dark about his son all this time."

"It wasn't your secret to tell," another woman remarked as she joined them in the bride's dressing room of the Little White Wedding Chapel that Parker's mother owned. After petting the dog that was overjoyed to see her, she held out her hand as Nikki had. "I'm Stacy Koz—Stacy Payne," she corrected herself with a chuckle. "Logan's wife."

Nikki laughed. "I still can't believe that one. I don't know which one is harder to believe, though—you and Logan getting married or Parker getting married…."

"Me and Logan," Stacy easily replied. "I saw Parker's house before it nearly blew up—it's a family house."

Nikki shook her head. "He uses it to fool women into thinking that he might actually get married."

"He *is* getting married," another woman chimed in as Mrs. Payne bustled into the room. "And very soon…"

"Where's Ethan?" Sharon asked, alarmed that the

woman who had taken her little man from her no longer had him.

"He's with his father," Mrs. Payne said.

And that reminded Sharon why she was marrying the playboy—so that Ethan wouldn't be taken away from her.

Mrs. Payne smiled. "All the guys are getting into their tuxes."

"I'm dressed now," Sharon pointed out. "I can take him back."

Mrs. Payne stepped forward and fussed with the veil, pulling it back over Sharon's face. "You're so beautiful. We can't have the baby messing with my new daughter's hair and veil."

My new daughter...

Sharon was grateful for the concealment of the veil now as it hid the tears that Mrs. Payne's sweet remark had springing to her eyes. She had claimed not just Ethan as family but Sharon, too. Sharon had never really had a family.

"I may step into the groom's quarters," Nikki said. "I'd love to see Parker wrestling a baby into a tuxedo."

"I already dressed Ethan," Mrs. Payne said. "And Logan is holding him while Parker dresses." She turned toward Stacy. "He looks very comfortable with a baby."

Stacy laughed. "You just talked us into getting married. Give us some time before you go looking for more grandbabies."

"You've already got one more than you thought you had," Nikki pointed out.

Mrs. Payne grinned. "Having him makes me want more."

Sharon had no intention of even consummating this

marriage, let alone procreating. "Mrs. Payne, are you sure we should be getting married in your beautiful chapel?"

"We already had one wedding at the hospital," she said with a glance toward Stacy.

Stacy smiled with pure happiness. "Logan couldn't wait another minute before making me his wife, and he wanted Parker to be his best man."

With the hit out on them, Parker and Sharon could wind up back in the hospital at any time—in a bed or the morgue.

"So we could get married somewhere else," Sharon suggested.

"It would break my heart if you got married anywhere else," Mrs. Payne replied.

But it would break Sharon's heart if something happened to the old church that the older woman had painstakingly restored and made into her livelihood.

But that didn't mean that there weren't other dangers out there. Sharon tentatively touched the lace gown. "And me in your beautiful gown?"

Stacy shook her head in amazement. "How has that same dress fit all the Payne brides? We're all different heights and sizes."

Stacy was shorter than Sharon and much curvier. "You wore this dress, too?"

Stacy nodded. "At the hospital. I was nervous to wear it, too, and changed quickly."

"It's Mom's magic dress," Nikki remarked.

Mrs. Payne gave an unladylike snort of derision. "It's a needle and thread and different-sized heels. And of course, beautiful brides that make it look so perfect…." She turned toward Nikki as if studying her to figure out the next round of alterations.

Nikki shook her head. "Oh, no! Don't even start looking at me like that…." She pointed at her mother and addressed Sharon. "See, I told you—"

"I was talking about the danger that Parker and I are in," Sharon reminded the others. "We've had people try to blow up the places we live or visit. I don't want anyone blowing up your chapel to get to us." And if the chapel blew up, the dress was sure to be destroyed…along with Sharon and her groom and everyone else in their wedding party.

"Cujo hasn't found any explosives. And all of the Payne Protection Agency is here," Nikki said. "You've never been safer than you are right now."

But as she walked down the aisle toward her groom standing at the altar, Sharon didn't feel safe. Not when she saw how tenderly he held the tiny boy who, also clad in a black tuxedo, was a perfect miniature of him. She felt a terror that she hadn't felt since she was a kid.

And if it wasn't fear for her life, was it fear for her heart? Was she afraid that she was going to lose it to the man she was about to marry?

God, she is beautiful….

Parker had been told that Sharon was wearing his mother's dress—the same dress that all the other Payne brides had worn. But his memory must have still been screwed up because he couldn't remember ever seeing anyone else in that concoction of white lace and silk. It looked as if it had been made for her alone—for her long, slender body. But it fitted and highlighted the curves that the ugly tan suit had hid.

She walked alone down the aisle on which so many other brides had clutched the arm of a father or a brother.

She had no one...but Ethan, who wriggled with excitement in his arms as he caught sight of the woman who had been more of a mother to him than his biological mother had. As she drew nearer, Parker forgot to breathe—until one of Ethan's flailing arms caught him in the jaw.

Even with the veil covering her face, the little boy knew who she was—and he wanted to be in her arms. And Parker was surprised that the boy wasn't the only one—Parker wanted her arms around him, too. But even more, he wanted to hold her—to keep her safe. He was so distracted by the sudden onslaught of wants and needs that the little boy managed to wriggle loose enough to lean toward Sharon.

As she lifted her arms to catch him, she nearly dropped the bouquet. But Nikki caught it before it hit the ground. Then, as she stood there with it clutched in her hands, Nikki's eyes widened in horror and she shook her head. "This doesn't count...." She slid back into the pew next to their mother, whispering, "This doesn't count, Mom...."

Light laughter rippled around the church at his sister's reaction. And usually Parker would have laughed the loudest before adding some additional comments. But he was too stunned by the beauty of his bride to be amused by anything.

But then Ethan tugged at Sharon's veil. And he laughed at the little boy's determination to get his hands in her hair. Parker reached out and lifted the veil over her face. It wasn't the time. He was supposed to do that at the end of the ceremony—before he kissed her. But he couldn't wait to see her face. And when he saw her face flushed with color, and her caramel-colored eyes sparkling, he couldn't wait to kiss her.

But he resisted temptation—just as Ethan resisted

the wrong idea. He had decided so long ago that he would never let himself love anyone and he doubted he could change now. But then again, he had gotten married....

His mother had gone all out despite his pleas that she not do that. Besides the dress and the ceremony and the rings, there was a reception. Food, cake, dancing...

He folded his arms around his bride, holding her close, while music played softly around them. His hips brushed hers and his body tensed, aching for her. He wanted to be alone with her, away from all the watchful eyes of his family, which was also hers now. But maybe it was better if he wasn't alone with her....

She stared up at him, her eyes dark and dazed, as if she was as surprised and overwhelmed by her desire as he was by his. They definitely should not be alone.

But his mother walked up to them, a sleeping baby in her arms. "You two should leave now," she said. "I will take care of him for the night."

Sharon seemed startled at the thought, but Parker wasn't sure if it was because she was panicked over being separated from the child or over being alone with her new groom. "But what if he wakes—"

"He's going to have to get used to spending time with his grandma," said his mother.

He should have known this was where her matchmaking was leading. She had wanted her kids married so she could get grandkids. Well, he'd already done his part, albeit unintentionally.

"Mom, I appreciate everything you did to make this seem like a real wedding, but—"

"It *is* a real wedding, sweetheart," she said. And she patted his cheek with her open palm. "It is a real wedding. You have a license to prove it."

So the wedding had been real, but the marriage wouldn't be. He couldn't let anyone hurt Sharon—not even him. "Mom—"

She smacked his cheek again—a little harder—and leaned in closer to him to whisper, "The marriage has to look real, too, so a court can't challenge it."

What was she asking him to do?

"Just leave together," she suggested. Then she turned toward Sharon and patted her cheek, but gently. "You are as beautiful a bride as you are a person."

Sharon's face flushed at the compliment. But she shook her head, denying it.

But Parker realized his mother was right. Sharon's beauty came from the inside out. If he was alone with her, he might be the one in trouble. But as his brothers had already learned, there was no arguing with his mother. Amid a shower of birdseed and glittering confetti, she ushered them out the doors to the front steps of the church.

Parker kept close to Sharon—not just because he was so drawn to her, but because he had already nearly been shot on these very steps. Logan had thought that those shots had been intended for him, but they had actually been meant to kill Parker.

"We set up a perimeter around the church," Logan said. "Nobody could get near it. You're safe here."

"Maybe we should stay," Sharon murmured, turning back toward the baby clutched in his mother's arms. She started reaching back, but Parker clasped her hand in his and led her down the stairs. A car waited for them at the curb—someone had attached cans to the back bumper along with a sign that read Just Married.

Nikki stepped forward and pressed the keys into

Parker's hand. "It's safe," she assured him. "Cujo and I checked it out thoroughly."

He pointed toward the cans and the sign. "I see that...."

She grinned and then reached up and kissed his cheek. "Be safe...."

She turned toward Sharon and kissed her cheek, as well. "Be careful...."

Parker helped his bride inside the car, making sure her dress was all in before he closed the door. Then as he ran around the front of the car to the driver's side, more birdseed and confetti struck him—stinging his face. He laughed and ducked and slid behind the wheel. As he shut the door, more birdseed hit the window.

But his laughter died and his hand stilled as he slid the key into the ignition. Nikki had checked out the car, and he trusted her. But he wasn't just trusting her with his life; he was also trusting her with the life of his new bride.

"It's okay," Sharon said. And she put her hand over his and turned the key.

The motor sputtered and then turned over, revving as he gave it gas. He uttered a sigh of relief. His family had kept them safe. He waved at them as he pulled away from the curb. To keep other cars away from the church, a big truck blocked the end of the street. It pulled forward as he neared, and Candace waved from the driver's seat. Payne Protection had surrounded the perimeter. But once he passed her truck, he was on his own. He would have to make sure that they were not tailed. He wasn't bringing Sharon back to the condo, though. He had found another place—a place nobody else knew about.

So he had to make extra certain that they weren't followed. He had to stay focused on the mirrors, watching for cars. But his bride kept drawing his attention to the passenger's seat. She was quiet, probably because she was scared. Maybe she didn't trust him to protect her alone. Or maybe she was upset about leaving Ethan with his mother.

It was when he turned to assure her that everything was all right that he saw the black SUV. It wasn't behind them. It was coming right at them—blowing through a stop sign to slam into the passenger's side—into Sharon. The big SUV struck with such force that glass shattered and metal crunched and then the car spun, turning over and over—scattering those cans tied to the back of it across the road. Glass struck his face and metal smashed against his arm and his head. He fought to stay conscious.

But Sharon was not. Her eyes were closed and blood streaked down from a cut on her head. Was she unconscious or dead?

Glass crunched beneath shoes as someone rushed toward the car. He didn't believe it was someone coming to his aid—it was someone coming to make sure he could collect that reward for a double murder.

Parker reached for his gun, but the seat belt, which held him in as the car landed upside down, was now also holding down his jacket so he couldn't get to his holster. He had no way of defending himself and Sharon.

He may not have wanted to get married, but now that he had, he damn well wanted it to last more than a few short hours. And the whole purpose of marrying had been to protect his bride, not to get her killed. But it was probably already too late for him to save her.

Now he couldn't save himself, either.

Chapter Twelve

Gunshots blasted, rousing Sharon from unconsciousness. The windshield now lay in pieces that were scattered on the pavement beneath the upside-down car. She sucked in a quick breath of panic. The car had turned over—and over—glass and air bags exploding while metal crunched.

Ethan! Had his child seat protected him?

No, no...

Ethan hadn't been with them. Mrs. Payne had kept him for their *honeymoon.* How had she forgotten?

She must have hit her head. She lifted her fingers to it now and they came away sticky and stained with her blood. But the cut was the least of her concerns with someone shooting....

She had hesitated to turn toward Parker, terrified that he hadn't survived the accident. But she turned now, as more shots rang out, and she realized that he was the one shooting. That he had drawn his weapon from his torn jacket, and, bleeding and pinned in the car, he was defending them.

"You're awake," he said with a ragged sigh of relief. But then he asked, "Are you all right?"

She replied with honesty. "I don't know...."

"If you can move, you have to get out of your seat belt," he said. "We have to get out of here."

"How many are they?" she asked. She wasn't naive enough to believe the SUV hitting them had been an accident—it had been another attempt on their lives. And since the accident hadn't killed them…

So many gunshots rang out, ricocheting off the exposed undercarriage of Parker's vehicle. Maybe it had been a blessing that they had landed upside down because it was harder for the men to fire bullets inside the vehicle.

Before Parker answered her question, he fired again, and a man's body, dressed all in black, dropped to the pavement in front of the car. He joined another darkly clothed man already lying there in a pool of blood.

A scream burned in her throat, making her eyes water. But she held it in and tamped down the fear that threatened to overwhelm her. She had to be strong now.

So she steadied her trembling hands and reached for the seat belt. But the car door had crumpled against it despite the side air bag that had opened on her seat. If not for the air bag, she would have undoubtedly been crushed. She had to push her hand between the now deflated air bag and the jagged metal—wincing as the metal scraped her skin—before she found the mechanism and released her belt.

She dropped onto the roof of the car—which was littered with glass and blood. Whose blood? Just hers or Parker's, too?

Like her, she noticed, he had a cut on his head. But he must not have lost consciousness as she had, or they would have already been dead.

"My seat belt is stuck," Parker said. "You need to cut me loose."

Fear and helplessness overwhelmed her again. "How?"

"I have a knife in my jacket pocket," he said. "Can you reach it?"

She slid her hand inside his torn jacket. And as she did, he fired again. She flinched against the earsplitting noise. That was probably why he hadn't wanted to fight with the belt himself—he was too busy defending her. So she found the knife. And careful to not slice him with the blade, she hacked at the belt until it shredded and tore and finally freed her groom.

With a grunt, he dropped to the roof of the car with her. Because there wasn't much room in the crumpled space, their bodies touched everywhere. She waited for a rush of pain from all of her bumps and bruises and cuts, but she felt nothing but the heat of his body and the reassuring protection of his presence. With him—with her husband—she felt safe, no matter how much danger they faced.

"We have to get out of here," he said again. "But we have to be careful. We don't know how many are left…."

Left? Two of them already lay on the ground in front of the car. Were they dead or just hurt?

She didn't let herself care about their conditions. These were men who killed for money, who didn't care that they would leave a child alone in the world just as she had been left alone.

"Stick close to me," he ordered her as he crawled through the shattered windshield.

She moved to follow him, but the glass left in the frame caught the lace on her wedding gown—trapping her inside the wreckage. She couldn't follow him. And he wouldn't leave without her.

More shots rang out. Would Parker die defending her?

"JUST TEAR IT," Parker yelled at her, as he kicked away the weapons of the men lying on the ground. Their cartridges were spent or he would have grabbed them to replace his gun. He was about to run out of ammunition. He was down to his last clip, and when that was empty, they would be helpless to defend themselves.

"I can't rip it," she protested as if horrified. "It's your mother's dress."

The dress his mother had worn when she'd married his father. It should mean something to Parker, but he didn't care about it as Sharon seemed to. He cared only about Sharon.

But then she was sliding onto the pavement with him. She had freed herself the same way she'd freed him. She had been knocked out. She was bleeding. But she'd rallied.

How had he ever thought that she was fragile? She was definitely the strongest woman he'd ever known—and he had known some damn strong women. He tugged her down beside him, where he crouched behind the wreckage of the SUV that had struck her side of his car. Three armed men had climbed out of the wreckage and he'd dealt with them.

Regret flashed through him that he had taken lives. But the men had left him no choice. They would have killed him and Sharon if he hadn't killed them first. Ideally, he would have rather taken them alive, but he'd been trapped in his seat in an upside-down car. He wouldn't have been able to fight them, to overpower them—especially when he'd been outnumbered. Even now, he had no idea if there were more....

Then he noticed something. Their driver's head had gone through the windshield. He stared down at him, his eyes open but unseeing. He hadn't survived the crash like Parker and Sharon had.

"I didn't rip the dress," she murmured, as if he cared about the damn dress. "But I think I'm bleeding on it...." Her voice cracked with regret and fear...and probably the horrific memory of her mother's murder.

"Are you hurt?" he asked. When he'd asked her earlier, she hadn't known. He could understand that because he had no idea if he was hurt, either—if any of the shots fired at him had even struck him. Adrenaline rushed so quickly through his veins, it was all he could feel besides the concern for her safety.

"I don't think anything's broken," she said. "What about you? Are you hurt?"

He shrugged and winced as pain radiated from his shoulder to his neck. He probably had whiplash from the car flipping over, but it was the least of his worries now.

He heard footsteps—a lot of footsteps running on asphalt. More than one person was coming. Had there been another car of assassins following this car?

And his ammo was running low. He had lost at least one clip when he'd ripped his jacket to free his holster. The shells had dropped onto the roof and rolled away. He was going to run out of bullets. "Sharon, you said nothing's broken?"

"It doesn't feel like it," she said.

Which didn't offer him much reassurance. But she was a survivor. She wouldn't have survived twenty years ago if she hadn't been smart, and she wouldn't have survived all these recent attempts on her life if she wasn't resourceful.

"I want you to run," he ordered her.

"Where?"

"Toward the houses, through the yards—find an unlocked shed or a garage or basement—someplace to hide." Like her mother had hidden her all those years ago. He hated that he kept bringing up those tragic memories for her.

But she wasn't worried about herself because her only question was "What about you?"

"I'm going to cover you," he said. "And then I'll come find you." Unless he ran out of bullets before the assassins did….

But then someone from his family would find her. They would protect her as he wished he could. But he could only watch as she ran through the gathering darkness as night finally fell. But the darkness was no protection for her as her white dress glowed like a beacon, drawing all attention to her presence and the direction she had taken between the houses.

It was more likely that one of the assassins would follow her, that he would find her before she even had a chance to hide.

Damn it...

The sound of the footsteps, growing louder as the people came closer, drew his attention back to the street. He clutched his gun and raised the barrel and hoped like hell he had enough bullets left.

HER LUNGS BURNED as Sharon ran, and the skirt of the wedding gown tangled around her legs, nearly tripping her. Gravel stung the soles of her bare feet. She must have lost her shoes in the car—probably when she'd been hanging upside down. But she didn't dare stop as gunfire rang out again behind her. Should she go back and make sure that Parker was all right? Or would her presence only distract him?

He had defended them earlier. He had to be able to continue to defend himself. And then he would come for her once it was safe.

So she had to hide. She had to find a place where she would be safe until he came. He would be furious if she didn't, just like her mother would have been had Sharon come out of the cupboard where she had hidden her all those years ago.

Parker was a protector like her mother had been. She had worried more about Sharon's safety than her own. Parker was the same way; that was why he had stayed behind despite undoubtedly being outnumbered. And that was why he had told Sharon to hide.

She stopped running, but her bare feet slipped on the grass and she skidded across the lawn of someone's backyard. At least she assumed it was a backyard. It was so dark that she couldn't see much—and this house was dark, too. Nobody was home, or if they were home, they weren't awake anymore.

How late was it?

She could have tried the house, could have seen if one of the doors opened. But she didn't dare risk waking someone—someone who might be as armed as the assassins who'd just tried to kill her and Parker.

Instead, she continued through the backyard, tripping over flagstones and garden statues. And because they had such a garden, she wasn't surprised to see another shadow in the backyard—that of a shed.

She fumbled around in the dark, searching for the door with her hands. But all she found were the wooden walls, and jagged splinters dug deep into her palms. She winced, but that pain was nothing compared to her fear.

She wasn't afraid for herself; she was afraid for Parker. The gunfire had stopped. She hadn't run so far that she wouldn't still hear it if they were shooting.

What did that mean?

That he was already gone?

Pain and loss filled her, pressing down heavily on her chest so that she could hardly breathe—so that her heart could barely beat.

Her hands skimmed across trim. She had found the door. But she had to fumble around even more to find the knob. Her fingers jammed against the metal handle. She tugged on it; the door rattled but didn't budge.

Another clank echoed in the eerie silence. And she found the padlock holding it closed on the top of the door. The lock refused to budge, too, but the little hook through which the lock slid was loose. She dug a fingernail into the head of one of the screws and turned it. It was so stripped that it fell to the ground. Then she tore the hook from the wood and pulled open the door.

She hurried inside the shed, but not to hide. She wasn't going to cower and hide again. She had already done that too often in her life. This time she was going to fight. Finally. So she fumbled around in the windowless shed until she found something to use to protect herself.

And when she heard the footsteps coming toward her, she didn't wait for the person to shoot at her or grab her. Like swinging a bat at a ball, she swung the shovel out, hoping to make contact. Even with the shovel, she couldn't overpower a man. However, maybe she could knock him out.

But she missed.

The handle was caught, grabbed in a strong fist and wrenched from her hands, leaving her with no weapon. No defense.

This man was undoubtedly armed like the others had been. So, really, what defense was a shovel against a gun?

Chapter Thirteen

Parker held tightly to the shovel. And he exhaled a ragged breath of relief that the blade hadn't struck his head. She had swung it forcefully and wildly. And now she threw things that she pulled off shelves. But it was dark and most of them missed him.

"Sharon," he said. But she kept throwing things. So he dropped the shovel and grabbed her, pulling her flailing body into his arms. She swung her fists and feet, fighting him. "Sharon! It's me. It's Parker. It's your husband."

Her struggle stilled. And then she was crying and clutching at him. "You're alive!"

"Yes," he said. "And so are you…"

And he was clutching her back, pulling her closer so that he could feel her heart beat and her lungs breathe.

"You're alive…." He shouldn't have sent her running off alone. The minute he'd done it he had regretted it. And when he'd nearly shot his brother, he had realized that instead of sending Sharon to safety, he had sent her off alone to deal with whatever dangers awaited her in the dark. He hadn't realized that *she* might be the danger—with the deadly shovel she'd wielded.

Once he had identified the footsteps as belonging to his family, he had left them to run after his bride. He had been worried that he would find her cowering in fear. Once again, he had underestimated her. She was far stronger than he had given her credit for.

She pulled back and stared up at him, her eyes glistening in the darkness. “Who was running up when I left?”

“My family. They heard the crash and came running from the chapel,” he explained. He should have known they would have heard it and the gunfire, too.

She kept staring up at him. “What about the gunshots I heard?”

He flinched, remembering how close he had come to hitting Cooper. “It was nothing.” He wouldn’t have fired at all but he had seen Cooper’s gun before he had seen who was holding it. If he hadn’t worried that a shot fired from it might hit Sharon as she ran away, he wouldn’t have risked shooting so soon.

Sirens wailed as emergency units approached the scene. Parker wanted to keep his arms around Sharon, wanted to continue holding her. But she had been hurt; at the very least, she needed stitches for the cut on her head. Maybe a CT scan to make sure she didn’t have a concussion. He had to bring her back to the ambulance.

“We have to go,” he said.

She pulled back and nodded. “Of course…”

He led the way out of the shed, making sure he stayed between her and whatever might have been waiting for them in the dark. But she stumbled and fell against him. So he turned and lifted her up into his arms. And he carried her back to where all the lights flashed and sirens wailed.

What had taken them so long to come? Had no one reported the accident or the gunfire? Officers were there now, in full force, stringing yellow tape around the crime scene. He should have been carrying his bride over a threshold to a honeymoon suite; instead, he carried her across the crime-scene tape and headed toward the ambulance.

Paramedics were working on the men on the ground, but he didn't care about their injuries as he interrupted them. "My wife needs to be checked out," he said. "She was on the passenger's side of the car that took the initial impact of the crash."

The paramedic glanced up from the guy on the ground. The young man shook his head. "I can't stop working on this patient yet."

"He's beyond help," Parker pointed out. "She could have a head injury. She was unconscious for a while."

"Until the shooting started," she said. "But I'm fine now...."

"I still want you to check her out," Parker told the paramedic. "She has cuts and bruises, too." But hopefully no broken bones or concussion.

"You better do what he wants," Logan suggested. "He and his wife were the victims in this crash. The men you're treating tried to kill them."

Parker had thought he had killed the men. But if the paramedics were able to resuscitate them, he wished they would. He would like these guns-for-hire brought back to life to answer all the questions he had about who had ordered the hit on them.

But Sharon was more important.

The paramedic looked from him to Logan and back. "You're Paynes, right?"

His twin nodded. "I'm Logan Payne, and he's Parker. You should be aware that someone put out a professional hit on him and his wife, Sharon Wells."

The paramedic's eyes widened. "Sharon Wells?" As another paramedic continued to treat the man on the ground, he stood up and led Parker to the ambulance. He pointed to a stretcher in the back. "I'll check her out now."

Parker hesitated before releasing her. He liked the warmth and softness of her body in his arms, liked the reassuring beat of her heart against his and liked the whisper of her breath against his throat....

"Mr. Payne?" The paramedic questioned his reluctance. "I'll make sure she stays safe."

That was all he wanted—for her to be safe. That was one of the reasons, along with keeping Ethan out of the foster-care system, why he had married her. So he forced himself to lay her down onto the stretcher and walk away. But he didn't go far. He didn't trust the paramedic; he couldn't trust him or anyone else. So he kept his gaze on him as he rejoined his twin.

"Who's with Ethan and Mom?" he asked. He had to make certain that his son and the boy's grandmother were safe, too. They were probably the only members of his family who hadn't come running up to the scene of the accident. Except that it hadn't been an accident....

Someone had tried to kill him and Sharon. He blinked and could see behind his closed lids how the SUV had slammed into her side of the car. He'd thought he had lost her then.

"Candace is on protection duty," Logan replied. "She took them off to a safe house."

Nikki stepped over the crime-scene tape and joined them. "I let Mom know that you and Sharon are safe."

"I doubt we're safe," Parker said as he glanced back at the wreckage. The SUV driver had risked—and given up—his own life to try to take theirs. And the others had stepped right into the line of Parker's fire in order to try to shoot him and his new bride. These people were too desperate to kill him and Sharon to ever give up—especially since the person who wanted them dead kept raising the reward.

That amount of money might be enough to tempt anyone....

Parker pointed his sister toward the ambulance. "Stay close to Sharon. Make sure nobody harms her."

She nodded and hurried off, obviously happy to act as a bodyguard since Logan usually kept her tied to a desk at the office. He probably would have literally tied her to it if she hadn't fought him.

Even now, the oldest Payne caught their other brother's attention and pointed Cooper toward the ambulance, too. Parker was grateful for the extra protection on his bride.

"You should be in that ambulance, too," Logan remarked.

Parker nodded. He should have been protecting Sharon himself. "I wanted to talk to you where she couldn't overhear." She had already been through too much.

"I meant that you should have paramedics check you out, too," Logan clarified. "You were in that car." He glanced back at it and shuddered. "And you got shot at. Are you sure you weren't hit?" He patted Parker's torn jacket, checking for bullet holes.

Parker shrugged off his concern. "I'm fine."

"You're a hell of a shot," Garek Kozminski commented as he joined them. He had come running up with the others but must have made himself scarce when the police arrived.

Maybe Parker had been too good a shot since the paramedics had abandoned their efforts to resuscitate the men. But if he hadn't killed them, he and Sharon would not have survived. But if at least one of the men had been only wounded, he might have been able to learn who had put out the hit.

"Looks like a wall of Wanted posters at the post office," Garek remarked as he gazed around at the bodies lying on the pavement.

"You recognize some of these guys?" Logan asked.

"What, you think all criminals know each other?" Garek asked.

"No," Logan said. "There are too many criminals. But how do you know these guys are wanted?"

Garek shrugged. "I recognize a couple of them."

"From their Wanted posters?" Logan persisted.

Garek shrugged again noncommittally. "I'm not sure that they're wanted anymore. But if they're out already, they must have gotten some light sentences for what they'd done."

Some people thought he and his brother had received light sentences for the crimes they had committed. Parker glanced around for Garek's brother, Milek. They were usually together, but Parker hadn't noticed the more laid-back Kozminski. Maybe he had been worrying about trusting the wrong Kozminski. He glanced back at the ambulance, where the paramedic shone a light in Sharon's eyes. Nikki and Cooper stood close to the ambulance doors, watching her.

He breathed a slight sigh of relief.

"Well, you know Judge Foster didn't give them the sentences if they were light," Logan mused.

And Parker considered what he'd said. Criminals often held grudges against judges, so he could understand if one of them had killed Brenda. But why go after her nanny and her ex-bodyguard?

"We have a connection in the district attorney's office," Garek said. "Milek can talk to his ex-girlfriend. Amber is an assistant D.A."

Logan shook his head. "No, you should do it," he said, as if he was protecting Milek from having to talk to his ex. It must have been a hell of a breakup. "You know who they are...."

"True," Garek said. "I'll see if Amber can look into their cases and find out how they've been paroled already."

Logan nodded his approval of his brother-in-law's suggestion. Then he turned his attention back to Parker. "Now let's get *you* checked out."

"I'm fine," he assured him again.

"You nearly shot me," Cooper said as he joined his brothers. "So you meant to do that?"

"He nearly shot me, too," Logan said. "It's not personal. He's jumpy."

"He jumped on me," Garek chimed in. "Knocked me down the stairs and bruised my ribs." He grunted as if he was still in pain.

Parker felt no pain. Only concern. "Get back to Sharon," he told Cooper. "If anything happens to her, I'll mean to shoot you next time."

"Sharon sent me to get you," Cooper said. "She wants you to get checked out, too. She's worried about you."

"See," Logan said. "She thinks you need medical attention, too."

Parker shook his head. "I'm more worried about her. That's why I wanted to talk to you alone, Logan." The others didn't take his hint; they stayed to listen to what he'd wanted to discuss with his twin. "I want you to take her and Ethan away from here."

"The city?" Logan asked.

Given the amount of the reward, getting out of the city wouldn't be enough. "The state. Maybe even the country."

Garek nodded his approval and added, "But be careful which country you choose. It could be more dangerous than staying here."

Was there any place safe for them? Any place they could go where there wouldn't be people willing to kill them for money?

He had to catch the person who had put out the hit so that everyone learned that they wouldn't be able to collect any longer. Brenda was the key; she had done or said something that had put him and Sharon in danger.

But what?

Sharon knew her best, so she would be able to help him figure it out faster than if he tried on his own. But he would rather try on his own than continue to put her at risk like he had tonight. Marrying her hadn't been the answer. It had only let the would-be assassins know where to find them.

But how had they heard about the wedding? Only family and closely trusted friends had been invited. Who had let the word out?

"We'll figure out later where you'll take her and Ethan—" And for their safety, only Logan would know....

"And Mom," Cooper added. "She's not about to let her first grandchild out of her sight."

Parker was glad that his mother had the baby right now. If Ethan had been in that car, too...

He shuddered to think about what might have happened to the baby during the crash and after, with all those gunshots. It was a miracle that he and Sharon hadn't been hurt worse.

Sharon...

He turned back to the ambulance. But it was driving away, lights flashing. *What's going on?*

Had she been hurt worse than he'd thought?

Or was it worse than that?

That paramedic had acted strangely when Logan had told him who she was. He had obviously recognized her name. Had he heard about the hit? Was he going to try to collect?

Parker sprinted after the ambulance as it sped away. His legs burned as he ran, and thanks to the traffic and other first-response vehicles blocking the street, the ambulance slowed. He managed to catch up. He reached for the handle of the back door and his fingertips brushed over the metal seconds before the ambulance driver hit the gas and sped off again. Maybe the driver hadn't seen him.

Or maybe he had....

He stopped, gasping for breath. Cooper and Logan caught up with him. "Damn you!" he cursed his younger brother. "You were supposed to stay with her."

"Nikki's with her," Cooper defended himself.

That didn't make him feel any better.

"We can't trust anyone right now," Parker reminded them.

"You can't trust your own sister?" Cooper asked.

"He can't trust the paramedic," Logan said. "That's why I wanted you to watch her and Nikki." He cursed, too.

And Cooper added his own string of curses as he got angry with himself.

Garek Kozminski just shook his head as his brother,

Milek, drove up next to them. That was where he must have been; he'd gone back to get a vehicle since they had all run from the church. "And people think *our* family is dysfunctional," Garek told his brother.

"Milek!" Parker greeted the other Kozminski as he hurried around to the passenger's side of the vehicle. "You need to take me to the hospital right now."

"You're hurt?" Milek asked, his gray eyes wide with concern.

Parker shrugged. He didn't know and didn't care. "No. I have to make sure that ambulance really takes my… wife to the hospital."

"And if it doesn't?" Milek asked.

Parker reached a hand out the open window. "Hand me a weapon," he ordered his brothers.

Logan shook his head. "You can't leave. The police want to take your statement."

"Pretend to be me," Parker said. It wouldn't have been the first time they had taken each other's places. It wouldn't have been the first time someone had mistaken Logan for being him; that mistake had recently nearly cost Logan his life, though. Parker didn't want to put him in danger again. "Forget that—just tell them I had to go to the hospital. They can take my statement there."

Unless that wasn't where the ambulance was taking Sharon and Nikki. If it wasn't, then Parker would be too busy tracking down the paramedic to give anyone his statement. He couldn't lose his bride now….

Chapter Fourteen

Fear had Sharon's heart pounding fast and hard. She couldn't move her arms. She couldn't move her legs. She was trapped with no way to move, no way to escape. The walls were so close and the space so confining that she could barely breathe.

Hysteria rose with the fear, choking her as sobs threatened. But she couldn't cry because she couldn't lift her hands to wipe away her tears. And she couldn't betray her weakness again.

She had to be strong.

"Not much longer," a disembodied voice murmured reassuringly, "Mrs. Payne."

She tensed at the unfamiliar name. But it was hers now; it was what she had signed on the marriage license next to Parker's name. Sharon Wells Payne.

She was married now to a man everyone, most especially him, had always said would never marry. She was married to a notorious playboy. While she had dated over the years, it hadn't been all that often and never seriously. What had she been thinking to agree to this marriage?

What if he wanted to consummate it?

"Mrs. Payne," the voice said again, "please try to

relax. We need you to hold still so we can get accurate images."

She sucked in a breath, but it was shallow despite the oxygen being pumped into the MRI machine. And she held that breath until, finally, the machine released her, sliding her back out into the bright lights and warmth of the radiology room.

"Are you all right?" a woman asked.

But it wasn't the voice she had heard through the speakers inside the machine; it was her new sister-in-law. She hadn't left her side since joining her in the back of the ambulance. She even walked beside Sharon now as a medical tech pushed her, on the stretcher, back to a curtained-off area in the Emergency Unit.

"That must have been so hard for you," Nikki commiserated, "being in that small space."

Sharon swallowed to clear her throat; she was more choked up over the woman's sincere sympathy than her own fear. "I'm fine."

"The MRI will tell us that," Nikki said. "That's why the doctor insisted on it."

"That was because the paramedic overreacted," Sharon said. He hadn't needed to rush off to the hospital with the sirens blaring and lights flashing.

"He's not the only one," a man remarked, as he walked around the curtain with Parker. It was one of the two blond men. They looked as alike as Parker and his twin, but she didn't think it was the one who had broken into the condo. This man didn't exude the cockiness the other one had. "Your husband has been tearing apart this hospital looking for you. And that was after he tore apart the paramedic."

"You did what?" Sharon asked. But Parker only stared

at her as if he had never seen her before or as if he had thought he might never see her again.

Nikki smacked her brother's arm. "You didn't hurt that cute paramedic, did you?"

"I—I…" He paused and cleared his throat as if he'd been choking on emotion. "I thought he might have been trying to collect the reward."

"You thought he was going to kill me?" Now she understood his stunned look.

Parker nodded. "He got rid of Cooper and then took off with you and Nikki. He didn't even stop when I was chasing the ambulance."

His sister laughed. "You hate ambulance chasers, and now you've become one."

Parker hated lawyers? Sharon felt a twinge of regret before she reminded herself that she was not a lawyer yet. If she didn't pass the bar, she would never be a lawyer. But at the moment, the bar was the least of her concerns.

"He tried," the Kozminski brother answered for him. "But the police were chasing him. They caught us before we could leave the crime scene."

She had been at the hospital awhile—long enough for a doctor to examine her and long enough that she'd gotten on the schedule for the MRI.

"Did they arrest you?" she asked.

He shook his head.

"They want your statement, too," the other man replied. He extended his hand to her. "I don't believe we've officially met yet. I'm Milek Kozminski. I am the nice Kozminski—unlike my brother, Garek."

She shook his hand. "It's nice to meet you. And it was nice to meet your brother, too." She had appreciated his brother's warning, not that anything could have prepared her for the ambush after her wedding.

The wedding...

She glanced around for the bag of her personal belongings. "Nikki, your mother's dress—what happened to it?"

"It's here," Nikki assured her as she lifted the plastic bag from the end of the stretcher. "And it's fine. Stop worrying about the dress."

"But I know I bled on it, and I probably tore it, too. I tried not to—"

"She nearly got shot trying to save that damn dress," Parker remarked.

She gasped at his callous disregard for his mother's memories. "But it's your mom's dress. It's part of her history with your father."

A history that had been cut tragically short. They hadn't even made it to their twenty-fifth anniversary. But they should have had a golden wedding anniversary—and a seventy-five-year celebration after that. Sharon knew not to wish for an anniversary for herself—not with Parker.

"Technically, it's most likely my dress now," Nikki said. "Since all the other Paynes are married, that leaves only me to wear this thing. And since I'm not getting married—ever—Mom will have plenty of time to fix it."

"Never say never," Milek advised as he patted Parker's shoulder.

He had said never, and yet his hand had been steady when he had signed the marriage license.

"Thanks for the ride to the hospital," Parker told the other man.

"Is that my cue to leave?" Milek asked. He had obviously realized Parker was dismissing him.

"I really do appreciate all you and Garek are doing

for us," Parker said. "Can you check in with him and see what he's found out from your friend Amber—"

"Amber is not my friend," Milek interrupted him, his mild-mannered personality chilling to ice. Whoever Amber was, she was definitely not his friend.

Parker sighed. "I'm sorry. Your ex—the assistant district attorney. Garek is going to ask her about those men."

"Did any of them survive?" Sharon asked. Now that they were no longer shooting at her, she didn't wish them dead.

But Parker shook his head.

Was he upset that he had killed? Had he ever done it before? He had been a police officer and a bodyguard, so he probably had.

"Dead men can't talk," Nikki remarked with a sigh of disappointment.

"Those kind of men don't talk when they're alive, either," Milek said with another pat on Parker's shoulder. He really was the nice Kozminski. "I'll check in with Garek and see if he's found out anything from—" he swallowed hard as if he struggled to even say her name "—Amber and I'll let you know…."

"He has my new cell number," Parker said.

The other man left with a nod.

"Are you going to get rid of me, too?" Nikki asked.

"Sharon is going to need a change of clothes," Parker said. "She won't want to wear that wedding gown again."

She had nearly been killed in it, but she had also married a handsome groom in it. She had looked beautiful—for probably the first time in her life. The good memories would outweigh the bad.

"They'll probably keep her overnight," Nikki said. "The doctor's worried about her MRI results."

Sharon wasn't worried. And moments later the doctor pulled aside the curtain to confirm that she was fine. She could leave. But where would she go?

Her honeymoon was already over….

PARKER CARRIED HER across the threshold. Finally. And he didn't have to step over crime-scene tape. This place damn well better not become a crime scene, either. He had been beyond careful when he'd driven back toward the lakefront. He had changed vehicles twice and taken a circuitous route. The threshold over which he carried Sharon wasn't to the penthouse condo but to a small cabin.

A honeymoon cabin.

But he didn't anticipate a wedding night. His bride was so exhausted that he had unbuckled and carried her into the cabin without her waking up. The cabin was all open and therefore easy to secure. The only room inside it was the tiny bathroom; through the open door, he could see that it was empty—no killers hiding in the glass shower.

He turned back toward the living area. The big four-poster bed dominated the space. He carried her over to it and laid her onto the quilted comforter. But her arms remained locked around his neck.

"Don't let me go," she murmured sleepily.

"I'm right here," he assured her.

But she tightened her grasp around his neck and pulled him down with her onto the bed. "I only feel safe when I'm in your arms."

He could understand why she would say that, but she was wrong. She wasn't safe with him—not with how much he wanted her, desire rushing through his veins. His heart pounded, and his skin heated. He needed her.

But he would only hurt her. So he gently tugged her arms loose and forced himself to step away from the bed, to step away from his bride.

She sat up, and her hair tumbled down around her shoulders. Those thick tresses tempted him to tangle his fingers up in that silk—to tip up her mouth for his hungry kisses.

His body tensed with need. But he ignored his needs and focused on her. "Go back to sleep. You must be exhausted."

She touched her fingers to the bandage on her forehead. Nikki had told him that Sharon had needed ten stitches to close the wound that she'd been so upset had bled on his mother's wedding gown.

She shook her head. "Not anymore. How long did I sleep?" She gazed around the cabin as if trying to figure out where he had brought her. Since she had slept most of the trip, she had no way of knowing.

"You didn't sleep long enough," he said. Because awake and tousled from her slumber, she was too damn sexy—even in the hospital-gift-shop T-shirt and pajama bottoms Nikki had bought her. She also looked too young and innocent for him.

He took another step away from the bed. But that damn cabin that he'd thought such a safe place to hide was too small for him to escape temptation. Her scent filled the space; she smelled like sunshine and rain. She was a paradox—like sexy innocence.

"Are you mad at me?" she asked, her voice shaking a bit as if she was afraid of him now.

He shook his head. "Absolutely not." He couldn't imagine being angry with her. "You're the one who should be angry with *me*."

"Why?" she asked with confusion.

"I promised I would protect you," he said. He closed his eyes and saw again that SUV crash into her side of the car—saw all the glass explode around her as the car rolled over and over across the asphalt. "And I failed you…."

Soft hands touched his face, drawing him out of that nightmare. She stood before him now, on tiptoe, so that her beautiful face was nearly level with his. "You didn't fail me," she said. "You saved my life." She leaned forward and brushed her lips over his. "You saved my life…."

He had tried to resist her. He had tried to control his desire. But she had come to him. So he kissed her back. He kissed her with all the passion and desire burning in his heart for her.

She wrapped her arms around his neck and clung to him, her feet off the floor. So he walked with her backward—toward the bed. Then he laid her down, and when she pulled him down with her, he didn't resist. He covered her body with his. And he never stopped kissing her.

She teased him with her tongue, sliding it over his lips. He sucked it into his mouth, and then he kissed her back that aggressively—driving his tongue inside her mouth.

She moaned and tugged at his shirt. He had lost his torn tuxedo jacket sometime ago. Now he pulled off his holster and dropped it and the gun next to the bed within reach. She was already working his buttons loose when he just pulled the pleated shirt over his head and dropped it onto the floor, too. Then he lifted her T-shirt and peeled it off.

Her hair tangled around her face and shoulders, and he smoothed the thick tresses with his hands. Beneath the plain T-shirt, she wore a strapless white lace bra through which he could see her nipples.

"You are so beautiful," he said in awe.

She shook her head. "You don't have to do that…."

"Do what?"

"Lie to me."

His pride was hurt. "You think I'm lying to you?"

She nodded.

"I have never been anything but honest with you," he insisted, "so when I tell you you're beautiful, I mean it."

Color flushed her face. He couldn't tell if she was pleased or embarrassed—until she kissed him again. She kept kissing him, even when he undid her bra and cupped her breasts in his hands.

Then she squirmed beneath him and moaned. She wanted him as badly as he wanted her. Her passion fueled his. He pulled away despite her clinging to him and unclasped and dropped his pants. Then he tugged off her pajama bottoms. A lace garter encircled one of her slim thighs. He'd been supposed to take that off earlier, so he did now. With his teeth. And he made sure his mouth skimmed over her silky skin as he pulled it down her leg.

Her breath shuddered out in a ragged sigh. "Parker…"

But she was wearing a G-string, too, which was all white lace. So he moved his mouth to that and slid his tongue beneath it. She squirmed again, and then she was clutching at him as he played with her with his lips and his breath and his tongue.

"Parker!" She screamed his name as she climaxed.

His body ached to join hers, so he parted her legs wider and thrust inside her. Then he tensed, worried that he'd been too rough. Emotionally, she was tougher than he'd thought, but physically, she'd been through so much, too. She was bruised and battered. Had he hurt her?

She moaned.

"Are you okay?" he asked. To him, she was perfect. But maybe he was too big for her—too much. He tried to pull back slightly, but she arched and lifted her legs, locking them around his waist.

She shifted, taking him deeper, and moaned again. "It feels—you feel—so good…."

He wanted her to feel better. He wanted her to feel more pleasure than she'd ever felt before. So he took his time, thrusting slowly and gently. And as he did, he played with her breasts, teasing the tense points of her nipples with his thumbs and his mouth. She drove her fingers into his hair and pulled his head up to hers. And kissed him.

And as she kissed him, she cried out with pleasure. And she peaked again. He joined her in ecstasy, groaning her name, as he filled her. But even as their racing hearts began to slow, he didn't release her; he kept her clutched tightly in his arms. He didn't want any space between them—he wanted her touching him everywhere.

"Are you okay?" he asked again, as he skimmed his fingertips lightly over the bandage on her forehead.

She chuckled. "I'm better than okay."

"I'm sorry," he said. "I shouldn't have taken advantage of you. You've already been through too much." And he should have been focused on protecting her. Instead he'd lost himself in pleasure—in her.

"You didn't take advantage," she assured him. "I—I wanted it, too…."

Why? Was she falling for him? Concern for her heart

clutched his heart. He didn't want to hurt her—like he'd hurt so many others.

He cared about her—more than he ever had cared about anyone else. Maybe he was even falling for her. But they were in too much danger to think about forever—to believe in happily ever after. And even when the danger passed, he couldn't give her the future she deserved—one without heartache and pain.

He didn't want her to fall for him, didn't want her to grieve for him someday like his mother had his father. But then, his mother had never regretted her life with his father; she had loved the years they'd had together, the family they had made together.

He and Sharon and Ethan were family. Could he really be a father? A husband?

Only if he survived....

Chapter Fifteen

Sharon's hand shook as she lifted her finger toward the security panel. She could do this....

The judge's body was gone. It had been transported days ago in the coroner's van to the morgue. Not that it would take an autopsy to determine what had killed her. Her neck had been brutally broken. She shuddered over the violent way her former employer had died.

A strong arm wrapped around her shoulders and the warmth of his body chased away the chill. As always, she felt safe in his arms. But she couldn't believe what they had done, that they had consummated their marriage. Maybe it had all just been a dream....

But he touched her now, comforting her. With the comfort came the memories, of how he had touched her all over. Goose bumps lifted on her skin, and she shivered. But she wasn't cold—not with his arm around her.

"You coming back here was a bad idea," he said. "You've already been through too much tonight."

"Last night," she corrected him, because the sun was already up. It had come up while they had been lying in bed together, still wrapped in each other's arms.

She would rather be here than back there, embarrassing herself more. She had thrown herself at him. He had caught her, but he was a playboy, so he would have caught any woman who had acted like she had.

"And you couldn't have come back here without me," she reminded him.

He shook his head. "I can now. Nikki shut down the security system."

Because there was no one to protect anymore....

He pushed open the gate. Crime-scene tape was strung around the estate and they stepped over it.

"Even though you could have gotten inside without me, you wouldn't know where to look," she pointed out.

"Look for what?" he asked.

She shrugged. "Whatever someone else was looking for the night Brenda was killed." If only she knew what that was...

"Someone was looking for something at the body-guard's apartment, too," Parker said. And he shuddered. That crime scene must have been gruesome, too.

She was glad she hadn't been with him then. But she wished she hadn't been in the interrogation room, either, with Detective Sharpe.

"They must have been looking for whatever he was supposed to have taken from Brenda's," she surmised. "You think he killed her?"

He nodded. "She scratched his hands and arms."

Brenda would have fought. She had been a fighter; it was one of the things Sharon had admired most about her.

"You said her laptop was missing," he remembered. "I didn't see it at the bodyguard's place, either."

"Books were ripped apart," she said as they stepped inside the house again. She shivered. Maybe it was just because nobody had turned off the central air yet, but it was colder inside the house than it had been outside. "They weren't looking for her laptop in a book."

Parker nodded. "True. And everything was torn apart at her bodyguard's apartment—even the pillows from his couch. So what were they looking for?"

"Flash drive," Sharon replied. "Brenda didn't trust computers." She really didn't trust anyone, thus her need for bodyguards. But then, her murder proved she hadn't been paranoid; she'd been right—especially since Parker believed it was her bodyguard who had killed her. "She constantly backed up her work."

"Work?" he asked. "Are you talking about her court cases or that book she was writing?"

"She wasn't working in the courts," she reminded him. "She had taken her leave to work on the book. When she asked me to proofread it, Chuck was here."

"That's why someone would think that you might know what's in her book. Do you have any idea what was in it?" Parker asked.

"I never got the chance to proofread it," Sharon replied. "I only know what you know about her. I don't know what else she might have written about." Sharon had been envious of the life the older woman had led, of the successes she'd had. But she wouldn't have killed her over it. "Who would have killed her over her own life?"

Parker shrugged those broad shoulders that just hours ago Sharon had clutched as their bodies joined together. She had never felt such pleasure, had never felt so special. But that was just because Parker was an excellent lover; he was notorious for his skills. He had made her feel special, but she doubted it had been special to him.

He didn't love her, but despite thinking she would be immune to his excessive charms, she had foolishly fallen for him. She loved her groom—her husband. And that was why she had insisted on coming back to the judge's house. Parker was doing his part to make them safe; she had to do hers.

"Maybe she wasn't writing about just her life," Parker remarked. "Maybe she was including other people's lives—lives that had either impacted or had intersected hers."

Sharon shrugged. She couldn't see Brenda writing about someone else.

"I know she was self-involved," Parker said, as if he'd read her mind. "Boy, do I know she was self-involved. I still can't believe she didn't tell me about Ethan—that she used me."

"She chose you," Sharon told him. "She respected you. She thought you were a good man." And a good-looking one, too. "That you had integrity and intelligence and charisma." Brenda wasn't the only one who could see all those special qualities in Parker Payne.

But he shrugged off her compliments as if he didn't believe her.

The night before, he had forced her to accept his compliments, so she pressed him. "It's true. You are all those things." And so much more.

"I doubt Brenda wrote about me," he said. "Good things wouldn't drive someone to commit murder. She must have written bad things about someone to make herself look better."

That was something that Brenda would have done.

Following his logic, Sharon added, "Maybe she revealed some secrets she knew."

"Some secrets someone doesn't want revealed."

Sharon checked the usual places Brenda would have

stashed a flash drive. Her desk drawer. The pockets in her empty laptop bag. But someone else had already checked those. And Brenda had been too smart to hide a flash drive someplace where someone would have found it.

So Sharon searched the unusual places—the dirt in the plants and the trim around the doorjambs. Parker followed her lead, but they came up empty-handed.

"What do we do now?" she asked. "If someone had already found it, they wouldn't still be trying to kill us—would they?"

Parker shrugged. "They might if they think we know what's on it. Chuck heard her asking you to proofread the book."

"He also heard her telling me to take Ethan and hide for two weeks and that if I hadn't heard from her to bring you…" Her face flushed with embarrassment for Brenda. But she needed to tell him everything.

"To bring me Ethan," he finished for her.

"She didn't call him by his name," she admitted. "She told me to trust only you—no one else—and to bring you the *package*."

He cursed. "She called my son a package?"

She sighed; she didn't want to speak ill of a dead woman. "Brenda wasn't particularly maternal. I knew what she meant, but Chuck might have been confused."

"He might have thought you were bringing me something else," he said. "Like the flash drive. And that was probably what he'd told whoever had tortured him before he died."

She gasped in horror. "He was tortured?"

He nodded. "He must not have wanted to put you in danger." He touched her face. "I don't blame him for wanting to protect you."

That was why he had married her. "But I don't have the flash drive," she said. "She didn't give me anything to give—"

He held up his hand, silencing her as he reached for his weapon. Then she heard it, too—the knob turning and the front door opening...

Someone had either come to search the mansion again or they had followed them here to kill them.

"Returning to the scene of the crime again," a cocky voice remarked as Detective Sharpe stepped inside the den. The rookie cop was close to his side, like a dog on a short leash. Both of them held their weapons, both barrels pointed at him.

Parker didn't reholster his weapon. Not yet. His heartbeat hadn't slowed even after he had identified the intruders. In fact, it had quickened. He moved forward slightly, trying to step between Sharon and the questionable lawmen.

"What about you?" Parker asked. "Why are you here, Sharpe?"

"I have someone watching the place."

It was pretty obvious who that someone was—his nervous sidekick. "Why?"

Sharpe waved his free arm to indicate Parker and Sharon.

"You were looking for us?" And Parker's heartbeat quickened even more.

Sharon's breath audibly caught, too. She didn't trust the detective any more than he did. "Why were you looking for us?" she asked.

"You didn't give your statement about the accident last night, Ms. Wells," Sharpe said.

Parker snorted. “That was no accident. That was an attempt on our lives.”

“Yet the two of you are alive and four other men are in the morgue,” Sharpe said. “Seems like wherever the two of you go, people die.”

Maybe the detective should have taken that as a warning because Parker didn’t dare lower his weapon yet, not when both of theirs were still raised.

“Those men tried to kill us,” Sharon said. “Parker saved my life.” She drew in a deep breath and added, “And it’s no longer Ms. Wells. It’s Mrs. Payne.”

The detective chuckled, but he didn’t seem particularly surprised. “I guess I owe you both congratulations.” He focused on Parker again. “Especially you,” he said, “since now that you’ve married her, she doesn’t have to testify against you. She can invoke spousal privilege.”

“You can’t hold him responsible for what happened last night,” Sharon defended him. “Those men were going to kill us.”

“Or so you claim,” the detective replied with that snide smile Parker wanted so badly to wipe off the man’s pasty face.

“I claimed it, too,” Parker said, “when I gave my statement to the officers who were at the crime scene last night. They believed me. They had already talked to witnesses who had either been on the road or in the houses by the scene.”

Sharpe shrugged. “Those officers know you,” he said. “They worked with you or your brother or your father, so they want to believe what you’re telling them.”

“They’re good cops—honest cops,” Parker defended the men. He couldn’t say the same about Sharpe and his sidekick.

"The feds sent an agent to investigate the River City P.D.," Sharpe shared. "To make sure there is no more corruption than your father's partner."

Parker narrowed his eyes and studied the men. They were obviously nervous about that fed's arrival. "My father's partner had been retired for many years. His conduct—long in the past—wouldn't have triggered an internal-affairs investigation, let alone a federal investigation. What the hell's going on in the department?"

And who had reported it? Judge Brenda Foster? Maybe she had sent that flash drive to someone in the bureau or the Justice Department. Was that what she had been writing about—police corruption?

Sharpe shrugged but didn't lower his gun. "Maybe they're investigating you."

Parker snorted again. "I'm no longer with the department."

"But you and your brother still have friends there—too many friends that might look in the other direction and cover for you," Sharpe said. "That's why I wanted to speak to you myself."

"Why not call me down to the station?" Parker asked. "Or go by the offices of Payne Protection to find me? Why track me down here?"

"I figured you would come back," Sharpe said, "to the scene of perhaps your first crime…."

"Criminals really don't return to the scenes of their crimes." Sharon spoke now. "I've studied enough court cases to know that's not true." She narrowed her big eyes and glared at the detective. "*You* know we're not criminals."

Almost too casually Sharpe asked, "Then why did you come back here?"

The guy was such an idiot that he thought everyone was as stupid as he was. But Parker had had enough of the games, so he answered honestly. "I expect for the same reason that the two of you showed up here."

"What reason are you talking about?" Sharpe asked, the snide smile slipping away to reveal his obvious nerves as sweat beaded above his upper lip.

"You're looking for the judge's flash drive," Parker replied.

The rookie glanced up at Sharpe, who betrayed himself with a widening of his eyes. Sharon had been right about the judge backing up her book on a flash drive, and that drive was exactly what someone was looking for.

He just hadn't expected that someone to be Detective Sharpe. What secrets could that kid have to hide? His incompetence? His ignorance? Those secrets had come out the minute he had opened his cocky mouth. But was there something else? Something he was worried that the fed might uncover in his investigation?

But even if the judge had dirt on Sharpe, the young detective didn't have enough money to offer the reward that had been offered for Parker's and Sharon's murders. He was the son of a single mother, who was the chief of police's younger sister—not heir to millions like Sharon.

"What flash drive?" Sharpe asked. "I don't know what you're talking about…."

Parker chuckled. "You know exactly what I'm talking about. I can see it on both your faces. Too bad I never played poker with either of you. I feel like I could have made some money off you." He turned toward the younger cop, who was obviously more nervous as his gun began to shake. "Is that what you're getting out of this? Money?

Were you supposed to kill me the other night—at the bodyguard's apartment?"

The kid shook his head, but his face flushed a bright red, revealing his guilt.

"Could you have done it?" Parker wondered. "If my brother hadn't shown up, could you have pulled the trigger?"

Maybe he did it to prove a point or maybe because Parker had scared him too much, but the kid squeezed the trigger now. And a shot rang out....

SHARON FLINCHED. But no bullet struck her. Then she turned toward Parker, and he stood straight yet. There was no blood spreading across his white shirt. "Did he hit you?"

Parker shook his head. "Guess I shouldn't have worried about you hitting me the other night."

Sharpe snorted his disgust. "Obviously you don't have to worry about him, but I'm a much better shot."

Or he was actually a killer, and the rookie hadn't been able to bring himself to actually kill. That was why he had missed. Not out of incompetence but decency. At least she hoped he had some decency. She had no such hopes for Sharpe.

Scared that he was about to pull the trigger now, Sharon screamed. "Wait!"

The detective paused and focused on her, waiting for her argument. She had hated the mock trials in law school. Put on the spot, she had always choked. Maybe that was why she hadn't passed the bar; anytime the pressure was on, she failed. Except for last night...

She had cut Parker out of his seat belt and helped him escape the wreckage. But the bravest thing she'd probably ever done had been making love with him and falling in love with him. And because she loved him, she would do anything to protect him. "Don't you know that Brenda always made several backup copies? I'm sure her lawyer received one upon her death."

Sharpe shook his head. "I already talked to her lawyer. How do you think I found out about you getting guardianship of her kid?"

"You looked that thoroughly for her flash drive," Parker remarked.

And she knew what he was thinking. If Sharpe had looked that hard, he would have found it—if it were to be found.

"You wasted your time," Sharon said.

"You just said she backed up everything," Sharpe reminded her.

"Yes, but if she only made one flash drive, I already have it." It was obviously what everyone thought, or there wouldn't have been a reward for her murder.

"Give it to me, then," Sharpe ordered, and he turned the gun on her.

As she stared down the barrel of his weapon, she swallowed her nerves and continued her bluff. "I have given that flash drive to someone else," she said.

"Who has it?"

"Logan has it," Parker answered for her. "And if anything happens to either of us, he'll open it."

Sharpe laughed. "Nice try. You wouldn't have been here looking for the flash drive if you actually had it."

"If we don't have it," Parker said, "why has someone put out the hit on us?"

Parker had flustered the young officer again because he kept glancing from Parker to the detective as if he didn't know whom to believe or whom to trust. Sharon tried to catch the kid's attention, so that she could silently implore him to help them. But like most of the men she'd met, he never looked her way.

Sharpe shrugged. "Maybe because they think you know something about the book she was writing."

Sharon exchanged a quick glance with Parker. She had been right; it was all about the book. She nodded. "Of course I know about the book," she replied. "Brenda asked me to proofread it."

"So you read it?"

She hesitated because she had never been able to lie. But she could stall. "She's not done with it yet." And if that were true, it would never be finished now. "She started it on her maternity leave and just took vacation to complete it."

"Have you read it?" he repeated.

"Not all of it," Sharon lied. Not any of it. "But I had the flash drive, so of course I looked at it."

"What is the book about?" Sharpe asked.

"It's Brenda's memoir," she replied. "It's about her life… and the people who've crossed her path over the years."

"Which people is it about?"

She hesitated again. *Should she say cops or criminals?* She glanced to Parker, but he only shook his head.

And Sharpe cursed. "You don't know a damn thing. You haven't read the book. So you don't have the flash drive, either—that's why you're here now. You're looking for it, too."

"Wh-what do we do now?" the young officer asked in a nervous stammer.

"I kill her and you kill him," Sharpe replied just before he pulled the trigger.

Sharon flinched again—waiting for the flash of pain, waiting for death…

There was no time—no time to tell Parker that she loved him.

Chapter Sixteen

While Sharpe had pulled the trigger, he hadn't done it as quickly as Parker had. The detective dropped to the floor. And instead of Sharon screaming, the young officer screamed and tried to steady his gun to fire.

Instead of shooting him, Parker just leaped forward and knocked the kid to the floor beside the detective. The kid screamed again and lost his grip completely on his weapon. Parker pulled it from his grasp and handed it to Sharon. He trusted her more with the gun than he did the kid.

She also bent down and retrieved the detective's weapon. She hadn't needed to worry about it. He was dead. But if Parker hadn't shot to kill, Sharpe might have struck Sharon with his bullet. Instead it had fired into the floor when Parker had dropped the detective.

"I—I thought he shot me," she murmured. And she was trembling but only slightly. She was tough. And smart. Her bluffing had bought them some time.

"Are you all right?" he asked.

"Yes, I'm fine," she said. "He didn't hit me."

Parker knew a bullet hadn't hit her. But she had to have been shaken by how close she had come to getting shot.

"Are you okay?" she asked.

"No, I'm mad as hell," he said. "I'm sick of getting shot at." The kid squirmed beneath him, and Parker tightened his grasp. The kid began to sob, his tears wetting the sleeve of Parker's shirt, as he held his arm beneath the young cop's chin. "Tell me who's behind the hits on me and Sharon."

He shook his head, or tried to, but Parker kept the pressure against his jaw. "Sharpe told me I had to help him, that I had to..."

"Kill me?" Parker asked.

He tried to nod.

But Sharpe had no reason to kill him—unless he had just needed the money. "Who was paying Sharpe?"

The tears kept coming, and the kid just shook his head. "I don't know. I don't know...."

Parker believed him. The rookie officer wasn't going to be able to help them find out who was behind the hits. So Parker eased back a little, still keeping the kid on the ground. Then he took out his cell phone but hesitated before punching in 911. Could he trust them?

But he had no choice. He wanted the young officer arrested. Maybe the kid would reveal more to authorities than he had revealed to Parker. But he doubted that the young man knew anything else. So he punched in the numbers and said, "I want to report a—"

Before he could get out the words, the door burst open and armed officers rushed into the mansion. Sharon held the guns. "Drop them," he told her, just as a bald-headed officer did the same.

They might use her holding the guns as an excuse to shoot her. She bent over and dropped them onto the ground next to the detective's body.

"On the ground! On the ground!" An officer shouted out the order.

Parker dropped onto the floor, too, and Sharon lay down next to him.

"Hands behind your heads!"

He locked his fingers behind his head, and Sharon followed his example. But maybe he shouldn't have obeyed any of the commands. No matter how many officers had rushed the house, maybe he should have tried to fight them. Because now he was down, and helpless to protect Sharon and himself....

And if these cops were as dirty as Sharpe and the rookie, they were dead for certain—execution-style....

ON THE OTHER side of the bars, Logan shook his head. "I always knew it would come to this someday," he said. "I knew I'd wind up bailing you out of jail."

Parker glared at him. "If you bailed me out, why haven't they let me out yet?" He rattled the bars.

"I paid the bail," Logan insisted. "So you better show up to court."

"For what charges?" Parker scoffed. "Defending myself? Sharpe was going to kill Sharon."

"Then it wasn't self-defense," a deep voice remarked.

Parker and Logan both turned toward the person who walked down the aisle between the holding cells. In the dim light, he looked like Cooper, but his hair must have grown out some. Had he bailed out Parker, too?

"It wasn't self-defense," Logan agreed. "It was defense of another person. He was protecting his wife."

"A court will determine that," the other man said.

It wasn't Cooper. His hair couldn't have grown out that much. But he had the exact same blue eyes, the exact same features, and he was probably about Cooper's age. Maybe younger because he didn't have as many fine lines on his face but a deep furrow between his dark brows.

"You're not Cooper," Logan said, and his eyes widened with shock. He must have done the math, too. If this man was younger than Cooper but obviously a Payne…

"Who the hell are you?" Parker asked. He hoped a figment of his imagination. This guy couldn't be real. It wasn't possible.… He reached through the bars and pinched Logan to see if this was real.

And Logan yelped and glared at him. "What's wrong with you?" But from the look of shock on his face, the same thing was wrong with him. He was as floored as Parker was.

But just because the man looked like them didn't mean that he was really related to them. The theory was that everybody had a twin in the world; of course, Parker already had one. So who was this guy?

Ignoring their interaction, the man replied, "Federal agent Rus."

"Russ?" Parker asked. "Don't you have a last name?"

"Rus is my last name," the agent replied. "Nicholas is my first name."

Their father's name…

The guy couldn't look that much like him and Logan and Cooper and not be a Payne. But their father had been an only child. So this guy couldn't be a cousin. Then that made him evidence of something Parker would have never believed: his father's betrayal. He couldn't deal with that right now—not with everything else going on in his life. Not with his life and Sharon's being in imminent danger.

"Who the hell are you?" Parker repeated.

"I'm here to investigate the River City Police Department," he said. "I'm acting as IA." Internal Affairs.

"Then you should know that Sharpe was dirty," Parker replied. "If I hadn't killed him, he would have killed me and my wife."

"As I said, a court will determine that, Mr. Payne."

"So you're not dismissing the charges?" he asked, incredulous. "That rookie cop was bawling his eyes out and announcing his guilt to everyone who would listen." That was why he was surprised that he and Sharon had even been arrested and booked. There should have been no charges. "*You* wanted us arrested," he realized.

"There can be no appearance of favoritism just because you're a Payne."

"Are *you?*" Logan asked, his voice gruff with dread and outrage. He had obviously come to the same realization that Parker had: their father had betrayed their mother. Their mother, who had loved and mourned the man for so many years…

"My name is Agent Rus," the man repeated.

"But are you our father's biological son?" Logan persisted.

The man shrugged. "I don't know. And I don't care. It doesn't make any difference to me."

But Parker suspected that Agent Rus cared very much and had made this persecution personal. He probably resented the hell out of his father's legitimate children. Pain grasped and twisted his heart.

How could his father have done this to their mother? It would destroy her to learn of his betrayal.

"I paid my brother's bail," Logan said. "Why haven't you released him?"

"I wanted to talk to you first."

"You wanted to rub it in our faces," Logan remarked, his usual cool composure slipping.

"Rub what in your faces?"

The fact that their father had not been the man they had always believed he'd been. How could he have betrayed his loving and loyal wife?

Parker was glad now that he hadn't confessed his feelings to Sharon. Knowing what he knew now about the man he had spent his whole life idolizing and respecting, he had proof that he couldn't be a good husband or father—not when Nicholas Payne had failed at it.

Sharon deserved better than him. She deserved better than a Payne.

SHARON HAD THOUGHT she'd met all the Paynes. And they had all been so nice. But this man—despite looking so much like Parker—was nothing like him. He wasn't warm and protective. He was accusatory and cold.

"Who are you?" she asked, confusion muddling her mind. She wrapped her fingers around the bars, gripping them. "I don't know you...."

All the Paynes had been so warm and welcoming to her. This man's eyes—the same sparkling blue as the rest of the Payne males—were icy. He looked about Cooper's age, but his hair was longer and his face meaner.

"My name is Nicholas Rus," he replied. "I'm a federal agent on loan to the River City Police Department."

He was the man that Sharpe and the young officer had mentioned—the one sent to clean up the police department and flush out the corrupt cops.

She breathed a sigh of relief. "That's good. You know, then, that Sharpe was a killer."

"Who did he kill?" he asked.

"Well, I don't know for certain but maybe Brenda Foster's bodyguard." She gripped the bars more tightly to still her sudden trembling. "And he would have killed me if Parker hadn't shot him first."

"Parker Payne has shot a lot of men over the past couple of days," the agent remarked as if making a casual observation. But there was suspicion in his blue eyes.

"Men who were trying to kill us," she said in defense of her husband.

"The convicts, maybe," he said with a nod of agreement, "but a detective and an officer…?"

"Sharpe was a criminal, too," she said. "And so is that young officer." The kid wasn't dead. In fact, he had confessed his involvement and Sharpe's guilt to the other officers who had arrived at the scene.

"Isn't that why you're here?" she asked. "To investigate the police department?"

He shrugged his shoulders, which were as broad as Parker's. He looked exactly like a Payne. Who was he really? Was it Cooper or Logan playing some game with her?

Could she trust anyone anymore? She couldn't trust the police—Detective Sharpe had proved that to her. And this man made her wonder if she dared to trust a Payne. How could he look so much like them but act as cold as a stranger?

"I'm here to ask you some questions," he said.

"I've already been questioned." And then she had been booked and charged on suspicion of everything—murder, manslaughter, interfering in a police investigation. Would she ever get out? Would she ever see Ethan again?

Her arms ached to hold her little man. But he was not the only one her arms ached to hold….

She shouldn't have insisted she and Parker go back to the judge's house this morning. She should have stayed in bed with her husband, in his arms…

She had been afraid then of falling in love with him and embarrassing herself. But she'd already learned twenty years ago that there were far worse things than embarrassment. There was death. And she and Parker had barely survived this latest attempt on their lives.

"I'm here to ask you about the flash drive that Brenda Foster gave you," the agent continued.

She had been right not to trust him. All anyone cared about was that damn flash drive. "If Brenda gave me a flash drive, it's been destroyed."

But *had* it been destroyed? If Brenda had given her a flash drive, she would have put it where she thought Sharon would find it. And suddenly she knew exactly where it was. Brenda hadn't just referred to Ethan as a package; she'd included his things.

The man tensed. "What do you mean?"

She couldn't trust him with the truth, especially not when she might endanger more innocent people. And no one was more innocent than Ethan and Mrs. Payne.

"It would have been in my things," she said, "my things that blew up in the hospital parking lot after someone detonated a bomb in my car." But there was one thing she'd had with her in the hospital—one thing that hadn't blown up. It had to be there….

He nodded, as if he remembered hearing about it. Or maybe he remembered setting that damn bomb. "So there's no way of knowing what the judge actually wrote—what might have been on her laptop or the mysterious flash drive?"

Sharon shook her head. "I don't know. She asked me

to proofread it when she was done, but then she sent me away to hide with her son. And I never saw any of her book." She glared at the man. "So nobody has any reason to try to kill me or Parker Payne."

The man's mouth curved into a very slight smile, which would have been unnoticeable except for the faint warming of his eyes. "I'm not here to kill you, Ms. Wells. I'm here to release you. Someone's paid your bail."

Parker. Or his family. They hadn't forgotten about her. But she didn't see any of them when the holding-cell doors slid open. Instead, she saw an older man waiting for her in the hallway. The agent walked away without another glance at her or at the stranger who had paid her bail.

"Sharon," the older man greeted her. "It is so wonderful to see you again."

Again? When had she seen him last? She cocked her head, trying to place the man with the iron-gray hair and dark eyes.

"The last time I saw you was at your grandfather's funeral. I am—I was—a friend of his as well as a colleague." He extended his hand. "Judge Albert Munson."

She nodded. "Of course. It's great to see you again." Heat rose to her face with embarrassment that she'd been arrested. Her grandfather would have been mortified. "Well, maybe not under these circumstances."

"And I expect I'll see you soon at another funeral," he said. "Brenda Foster was also a colleague of mine as well as your employer," he explained. "Your grandfather should have asked me to hire you as a law clerk. You would have been safer working for me."

But then she never would have met Ethan and fallen in love with the little man and with his father. "I learned a lot from working for Brenda," Sharon said. A lot about how to love and what was important.

Family. Even though that family wasn't hers....

"But thank you for posting my bail," she said. "I will repay you as soon as I can get to a bank. I lost my ATM card and checkbook when my car was destroyed."

But maybe she hadn't lost what everyone was looking for—well, nearly everyone....

He nodded. "I have heard about the troubles you've been having."

Well, that was obvious. How else would he have known she was at the police station? He appeared to be nearly as old as her grandfather. Was he still on the bench?

She hadn't paid much attention to any judges except Brenda since she'd started working for her. "It'll all be over soon," she assured him. "I just need to speak to my husband."

She started out of the holding-cell area, toward what she assumed was the lobby, but the judge caught up with her and grasped her arm. Despite his age, his grip was surprisingly strong—almost painfully so.

"He hasn't been released," the judge said.

"Well, then I'll wait for him," she said. "I'm sure his family has paid his bail." He would have called them, or someone in the police department would have called his brother Logan for him. There were people they couldn't trust in the department—like Agent Rus—but there were also people who knew and respected the Payne family.

"How do you know it will all be over soon?" he asked.

She turned back and noticed the desperation in his dark eyes. And she realized whose secrets Brenda had been going to reveal in her book....

She shook her head. "I don't know...."

"You're lying," he accused her. "Don't perjure yourself, Sharon."

And then she felt it. Not only was he grasping her arm, but he was also pushing a gun into her side. She recognized the coldness of the metal barrel.

How had he gotten it inside the police department?

She glanced around, looking for help. But the agent who looked so much like Parker and his brothers was gone. The only person standing around was a young officer who opened a door for the judge—a door to a back alley. That was obviously how the judge had gotten the gun inside—with this officer's assistance.

"Help me," Sharon implored him as the judge pulled her into that alley.

But the officer just lowered his head and stared down, uncaring that he was probably sending her to her death. She had been bailed out, not ordered to be executed. Why wouldn't he help her?

"You're behind everything," she said. "You're the one who put out the hit on me and Parker."

"Maybe I should have let you wait for your husband," the judge replied. "Then I could have killed you both—together."

"Parker doesn't know anything," Sharon said. "He's never seen the flash drive."

"But you know…."

"I just figured it out now," she said. "Brenda never showed me any of her book. How did you even know she was writing it?" Brenda had been too smart to announce her intentions to the dirty judge.

Munson chuckled. "As you know, she treated employees like dirt. So her bodyguard had no reason to be loyal to her."

Parker would have been. She never should have fired him. But if she hadn't, Ethan wouldn't have been born, and Sharon couldn't imagine a world without him. Or without Parker...

"Chuck told you?"

The judge nodded. "He saw some of her research and offered me the information for a price."

"And you had him kill her and steal the laptop," she realized. "But then you had him killed, too."

"Before he died, he admitted that you were going to proofread the book for her," he said. "And he also revealed—under duress—that you were supposed to bring a *package* to Parker Payne if you hadn't heard from the judge. Horowitz had a soft spot for you, Ms. Wells. He didn't want to put you in danger."

The bodyguard had looked at her as everyone else who knew about her mother had—with pity.

"I used to, as well," the judge admitted. "You went through a lot as a child and then you had to put up with His Honorable Judge Wells."

She shivered at the coldness in the judge's voice and from the memory of her grandfather's coldness.

"But my soft spot hardened," Albert Munson continued, "when I learned that you know too much."

She shook her head. "I haven't seen the book. I haven't even looked at the flash drive."

"But you know where it is."

She sighed and nodded. Then he opened the passenger's door and shoved her inside the car. As he went around the hood to the driver's door, she tried her handle, but it was locked.

The judge glanced back toward the police department, as if considering. Then he opened the driver's door and slid behind the steering wheel. "Parker Payne really doesn't know anything about the flash drive or the book?"

"He thinks Sharpe was behind everything," she lied. She wasn't a good liar, but she was getting better at it since she was doing it to protect the people she loved.

Parker already knew that Sharpe hadn't had the money to offer the outrageous reward the judge had. But how had Judge Munson had so much money? she wondered. Her grandfather had been well-off, but most of that had been his and his wife's family money. Not just what he had earned as a judge and a law professor.

"Then Payne isn't as smart as Brenda thought he was," Munson remarked. "Your grandfather would have been disappointed that you married beneath you."

"My grandfather was always disappointed in me," she replied. But she didn't care what he thought anymore—which was amazing because even after he'd died, she had been trying to please him. That was why she had tried to become a lawyer. For him. But she didn't care about the past anymore.

She cared about the future. The future for Ethan and Parker. She needed to protect them...even though it was probably going to cost her her life....

Chapter Seventeen

Anger coursed through Parker's veins, making his blood pump fast and hard. He wasn't mad about the federal agent or even about being arrested, though. He would deal with all that later. Right now he was worried about his wife. "Where the hell is she?"

He couldn't protect her if she wasn't with him. And God knew they both needed protection—even in the police department. He had finally been released from the holding cells, but now he paced the lobby, refusing to leave until they released his wife, too.

Logan shrugged. "I've asked…."

But nobody had answered his or Parker's insistent questions. At least the desk sergeant hadn't and neither had the officers milling around. So he walked up to the desk again. "I want to talk to Agent Rus."

Behind him, Logan cursed. He obviously hadn't wanted to see the agent again. Maybe, like Parker, he wanted to forget that Nicholas Rus even existed. Apparently their father must have because he had died fifteen years ago without ever mentioning that he had another son, one around Cooper's age.

"I can't believe I am willingly walking into a police station," a male voice remarked.

And a female laugh rewarded his witty remark.

Parker understood why Logan had cursed when he turned around. Logan was rushing up to their mother, whom Garek Kozminski was escorting into the lobby.

"But then, you know I would do anything for you, Mrs. Payne," Kozminski told her, oozing his usual smarmy charm.

And *Parker* was the playboy?

He was a happily married man. Or he would be when he knew where on earth his wife was.

He was happy? Images flashed through his mind—images of him and Sharon making love—and he realized he had never been happier or more connected to another human being. Not even his son.

"Where's Ethan?" was his first question for their mother, though.

"Cooper and Tanya are watching him," she replied. Then her eyes widened with surprise as she peered over Parker's shoulder. "Or so I thought…."

"You asked to see me," a deep voice said from behind Parker.

He flinched. Even his mother had mistaken the agent for one of her sons. There was no way she wouldn't realize who he was.

She gasped. "You're not Cooper…."

"How the hell many Paynes are there?" Garek remarked. Logan punched his shoulder in reply.

Parker wanted to wrap his arms around her—wanted to protect his mother like he wanted to protect his wife. But she pushed him aside so that she stood in front of the agent. Then she reached up and cupped his face in her hands just as she always did her children.

But this man wasn't her child….

Didn't she realize that?

"You're Carla's son, aren't you?" she asked.

He didn't pull away from her touch even as he nodded. "You knew...?"

"I knew about your mother," she said. "I didn't know about you until right now." Tears overflowed her warm brown eyes, rolling down her cheeks.

Parker wanted to wipe them away. But before either he or Logan or even Garek Kozminski could reach for her, Nicholas Rus closed his arms around her. Then, his deep voice gruff with emotion he hadn't yet revealed himself capable of feeling or showing, he said, "I'm sorry...."

"You have no reason to be sorry," she said, as she closed her arms around him and hugged him.

"I should have done something so you wouldn't have been so surprised." He pulled away from her, evidently embarrassed by what Parker suspected was an uncharacteristic display of sentiment. "I should have warned you...."

To his credit, Agent Rus probably hadn't counted on her showing up at the police department. Neither had Parker.

"You don't need to be here," Parker told his mother. "I've already been bailed out. I'm just waiting to find out why Sharon hasn't been released."

"She has been released," Rus replied.

"But I haven't been able to pay her bail," Parker said. "Did you dismiss the charges?" He didn't care about himself; he cared only about Sharon. She hadn't even pulled the trigger; he had.

Rus shook his head. "Not yet, but I am working on it."

Did that mean he believed them? That they had only acted in self-defense?

"Then how did she get released?"

"Someone else paid her bail," Rus replied in a slightly patronizing tone.

But the agent didn't know that Sharon Wells had no one. Her family was gone, and the one person who may have been her friend had been brutally murdered.

"Who?" Parker asked.

"Judge Albert Munson," Rus replied. "He said he was a friend of her grandfather's."

"Al is a friend of mine, too," Mrs. Payne remarked. "He's the judge who helps me get the marriage licenses issued without the waiting period."

Panic clutched Parker's heart. "Did he issue mine and Sharon's?"

She smiled and nodded. "Of course. He was very happy to do it, too."

No doubt he had been because then he had known when and where they were getting married, and he had been able to set up the ambush that had very nearly killed them.

"Good ole Judge Albert is everyone's friend," Garek chimed in, "especially criminals'. The assistant D.A. informed me that Munson is the judge who either threw out or reduced the sentences of those guys Parker took care of and quite a few more…."

So there were more criminals out there with a debt owed to the judge. Or had they already paid him? Was that what Brenda had had on him—what she'd written about in her missing manuscript?

"Where is she?" Parker asked. "Where did she go after you released her?"

Rus shrugged. "When I left, she was talking to the judge. She was thanking him for bailing her out."

He was a friend of her grandfather's. She probably would have left with him without ever realizing the threat he posed. But why would she have left without Parker?

Hadn't last night meant anything to her? Maybe he shouldn't have been so concerned about her falling for him. Apparently she hadn't even cared enough to stick around to make sure he got bailed out.

But it didn't matter whether or not she loved him. He loved her. And he was going to damn well make certain nothing happened to her.

"Give me the keys to your car," he ordered Logan. His hand shook slightly as he held it out.

"You don't know where she is," Logan pointed out.

"I'll find her," Parker said.

"It's not safe for you to be running around out there alone," Logan said as he held on tightly to his ring of keys. "I'll drive you."

Logan wouldn't drive like Parker would—with the urgency necessary to find his wife before the judge hurt her. "You can ride along with me," he offered, his hand still held open between them, "but I drive."

The second Logan reluctantly handed over the keys, Parker was gone. He didn't have a minute to lose. He had to find his bride….

PARKER WOULD HAVE no place to look for Sharon. She had no apartment anymore. Not even a car. And since he didn't know anything about Judge Munson, he wouldn't look for her at his estate, either. So Sharon talked the judge into driving her back to Brenda's house.

And even if Parker didn't come looking for her like he hadn't at the police station, there might be someone else around—one honest officer at the scene—who would come to her aid.

"It's not here," the judge said. "I've had too many people search this house for it to still be here."

She wasn't about to tell him where it really was—not even when he raised his gun and pressed it to her temple.

"Don't play games with me, little girl," he threatened her. "You brought me here because you thought there might be crime-scene techs or officers here."

But she had been wrong—as the judge had known or he wouldn't have brought her there. Everyone was gone. Only she and the judge stood inside the mansion where two people had already died. Was she about to be the third?

If only she could somehow get word out to Parker…

To warn him…

"It wouldn't have done you any good if there had been officers here," he continued. "Didn't you see the one at the station? He is on my payroll along with so many others."

She would have shaken her head but for the gun pressed to her temple. "There are honest cops, too," she insisted. "Cops you haven't been able to buy. And Parker will know who they are. He'll take the flash drive to them."

The judge snorted. "He might if he had it. But we both know he doesn't have it."

"He does," she insisted. "That's why I couldn't wait to see him—to find out who was behind these attempts on our lives. Now I know it's you…."

The judge shrugged. "It's not like you'll live to tell anyone anything," he said. "And even if you did, they would never believe you—not without the flash drive. I am as widely respected as your grandfather was."

She doubted that. If he was really known for his integrity, her grandfather would have had her clerk for this man. But Judge Wells had never really mentioned him.

"I'm even friends with your mother-in-law," Munson said with a chuckle. "She came to me for your marriage license. If not for me, you wouldn't be Mrs. Parker Payne."

So that was how those men had learned where she and Parker were the night they'd married....

He laughed again. "Not that you're going to be much longer...." From the corner of her eye, she saw that he moved his finger along the gun toward the trigger.

Was he going to kill her here?

Would Parker find yet another body in this house?

An odd ring, more of a chime, rang out—distracting them both. Sharon's phone had blown up in her car, and she hadn't had time to find a replacement. Maybe if she had, Parker could have traced it and found her.

But she had no way of leading him to where she was. She had no way of leaving a message for him to find the flash drive, either. If she tried, the judge would see it, and she couldn't endanger Ethan and Mrs. Payne.

The judge fumbled the ringing phone from the pocket of his suit jacket. "Don't try anything," he warned her. "Or I'll splatter your brains right now." He cocked the gun.

She swallowed hard, choking down her fear. She didn't want to die, but she saw no way out of her situation. No way to survive...

"Hello?" the judge answered, his voice full of suspicion. He must not have recognized the number on the caller ID. Then he chuckled. "Parker Payne, your wife and I were just discussing you."

He must have clicked the phone onto speaker because then she could hear Parker's voice, gruff with concern and anger and fear. For her?

Did he care about her? Did he love her? Or was he only being a bodyguard?

"Munson, you better not hurt her or I will not only give this flash drive to the feds but to all the media outlets, too."

The grin left the old man's face, and his eyes darkened with anger. "You are not the one who should be threatening me, Payne."

"I have what you want," Parker said.

"I thought she was lying," the judge admitted, "when she said you had it…."

Had Parker found it? Or was he bluffing like she had earlier?

"Sharon would never lie," Parker said. "She doesn't have it in her. She's a good person who's already been through too much in her life. She is the granddaughter of your friend. Don't hurt her."

"Looks like I have what you want, too, Payne," the judge replied with a sly glance at Sharon.

"You do," Parker said.

But he must've still been lying. He couldn't want her—not for more than the night before. He couldn't want her forever.

"Then perhaps we can work an exchange," the judge offered, as if he was being magnanimous. "Meet me at my estate in an hour, Payne. Alone."

"I won't give you anything if she's already dead," Parker warned him. "You better not hurt her…."

"I won't." The judge offered what for him was a pithy promise. Then he hung up the cell. "I won't kill you," he assured her, "until your husband brings me that flash drive. Then I'll kill you together."

He acted as if he were doing them a favor. But then, maybe he was. Sharon had spent so much of her life alone. But she would still rather die alone than have Parker die with her. But it was too late; she had no way of warning him that he was about to walk into a trap.

Chapter Eighteen

If only Parker had been able to figure out where the real flash drive was…or if it even still existed. There had been so many explosions; it could have been destroyed in any of them. But because he hadn't been able to find it, he walked into the judge's mansion with a blank one and hoped like hell he could bluff as well as Sharon had.

He held tightly on to it, refusing to give it up like he had his gun and his knife and his phone to the guards at the police station. Guards? He recognized some of the men as officers from the police department but most of them, like Garek had said, from Wanted posters. Or men who'd been on those posters previously…

How had no one else figured out what Brenda had? That Judge Munson had to have been taking bribes all this time. How many criminals had he thrown out cases against or set free before they had served their sentences?

Several of them surrounded the estate. Too many for him to overpower alone.

Judge Munson's estate was four times the size of Brenda Foster's, and an assortment of antique and classic cars were lined up in the circular driveway. The judge had obviously been living beyond his means, so he had found a way to supplement his income.

Two armed men pushed Parker down a wide hallway, lined with an Oriental runner, to a room in the back of the mansion. It was some type of solarium filled with plants and wicker furniture. Tied to one of those wicker chairs, Sharon looked fragile and fearful.

Rushing forward, Parker dropped to his knees beside her. "Are you all right?"

"She's fine," the judge answered for her. He stood in a corner of the solarium, a gun in his hand. With his iron-gray hair and complexion, he could have been a statue—he was that rigid and unemotional. "Where's the flash drive?"

"Don't give it to him," Sharon said. "He's going to kill us anyway."

The judge chuckled but didn't deny her claim. He obviously thought he had set a trap for Parker. "So you might as well give me the flash drive and get this over with."

Sharon shook her head. "Not yet. You were my grandfather's friend," she said. "So have some mercy. Let me talk to my husband."

"I wasn't really a friend of your grandfather's," Munson admitted. "In fact, I hated the man so much I only showed up at his funeral to gloat."

"He wasn't a good man," Sharon admitted. "He was rigid and disapproving. It was not easy being his granddaughter."

"Trying to get my sympathy?" Munson asked with a heartless chuckle.

Parker suspected that she was actually telling the truth—that her grandfather had not been an easy man to live with or please. And she had been a traumatized, vulnerable young kid when she had come to live with him and her grandmother. His heart ached for all the pain she had endured at such a young age. He wanted to hold her.

"Let us have a minute," Parker implored him. He wanted to talk to her, too, to assure her that he would figure a way out for them—that he already had a plan in place.

"Now, your mother I have always liked," the judge admitted. "Penny Payne is a good woman, when so few women are really good."

She was a better woman than Parker had even realized because she had spent the past fifteen years mourning a man she knew had betrayed her. With *Carla*...

"Then do it for my mother," Parker said, "since you're going to break her heart." Not that her heart hadn't been broken before—more times than he had ever known.

"Give me the flash drive," the judge demanded. "And I'll let you talk...."

Parker hesitated for just a moment before handing over the blank drive. The judge closed his hand around it and tightened his grasp on his gun. But then he took the flash drive and headed over to where a laptop sat open on a small table in the corner of the sun-filled solarium.

Parker crouched down next to Sharon and reached for the thin rope binding her wrists to the arms of the wicker chair. If only they hadn't taken his knife...

"I want you to know something," Sharon said.

Was she going to tell him how she felt about him? His heart quickened. But his attention was divided. Once the judge realized the flash drive was empty, he might start firing. Parker had to protect her; he struggled harder with the ropes, trying to loosen them. But he was only cutting the strong, thin rope into her delicate skin.

She flinched. "I want you to know how much I love..."

She drew his attention from the judge to her beautiful face. Her eyes were so full of fear and distress and another emotion.

Love?

She finished, "...Ethan."

Of course she loved the little boy whom she had cared for since his birth. Of course she wanted Parker to know that.

"I love him so much," she continued, "that I never even minded lugging that diaper bag everywhere with me." And her eyes spoke to him, passing the message along....

The flash drive—the real one—was in the diaper bag. The diaper bag that his mother had taken along with the baby.

The judge glanced up. "What a touching goodbye." Then he cursed. "There's nothing on this damn flash drive. You brought me an empty one!"

"You really thought I was stupid enough to bring you the real one?" Parker asked. "I know you intend to kill us. You wouldn't have put out the hit on us—and upped the reward—if that hadn't been your intention all along."

"Trying to get a confession out of me?" the judge scoffed. "I had my men check you for a wire. You're not wearing one. Do you think either of you are actually going to survive to testify against me?"

Parker shrugged. "If we don't get out of here within the hour, the flash drive will go to someone I actually trust in the police department—someone you can't buy." He didn't know if there was anyone he could trust within the department anymore—not after he had learned his father's partner had betrayed him. And now that he had learned his father had betrayed his mother...

The judge snorted in disbelief of Parker's claim. And he narrowed his eyes and studied Sharon. "Why did you tell him about the diaper bag? Is that where the flash drive is?"

The man was smart. Too smart.

"That diaper bag was in this house," he said. "Penny brought it with her when she got me to waive the waiting period and issue your marriage license." He stood up and turned toward the door, probably to summon one of his henchmen to send after their son.

Sharon gasped in fear, and she struggled against those ropes even harder.

"It's not in the diaper bag anymore," Parker said. "I found it already and took it out."

The judge shook his head. "Nice try. I don't even have to send someone to get her. I can call your mother and summon her here to show off that grandbaby of hers again. She'll be happy to do that—happy to bring along the bag."

Parker shook his head. "And you'd be wasting your time. I took it out already and I read everything that was on the flash drive."

"Prove it," the judge challenged him. "Tell me what's on it."

"I know that Brenda wrote about your taking bribes to throw out cases," he replied, "or at the very least to reduce sentences."

The judge tensed and the color of his face turned grayer than his hair; Parker's bluff was actually on the money. Because the judge had been all about the money....

"You saw it," the judge conceded. "You have it."

"Not on me," Parker said. "I gave it to my brother, who'll turn it over to someone we trust."

"That's the problem," the judge said. "You can't trust anyone." And he lifted his gun again. "I don't trust you, Payne. I'm not sure if you really read what Brenda wrote about or you just guessed it. Either way, you and your bride are going to die."

THE JUDGE WAS going to kill them. Sharon knew it now. She had hoped that somehow Parker would save them as he had so many times before, but she shouldn't have relied on him to protect them. She should have protected him and Ethan; he had already missed so many milestones in the boy's life—his first smile, the first time he had rolled over, his first crawl. He didn't deserve to lose any more.

Sharon whispered to Parker, "I'm sorry."

"You have no reason to be sorry," he assured her.

She had regrets, though. Regrets that he had come to her rescue—or tried. But that was the only thing she regretted about her time with Parker Payne.

"I know it's too late," she said. There was so much she wanted to tell him, that she wanted to share with him. But now whatever chance they might have had to make their marriage work was gone—like they would soon be.

He shook his head and squeezed her hand, offering her comfort right until the end. His efforts with the ropes had loosened them some but not enough for her to tug her wrists free. "Shhh, it's going to be okay."

But it wasn't. They were going to die. At least Ethan would have family, though—family who loved him like she loved him and his father.

Tears stung her eyes so painfully that she couldn't blink them back. She could only let them fall, like she had fallen for Parker Payne. "But I want you to know that I love you."

"Now, that was touching," the judge bitterly remarked. "Are you going to say the words back to her, Payne?"

Parker ignored the older man and stared at her. His blue eyes, those gorgeous blue eyes, filled with regret.

She had known he hadn't returned her feelings. But seeing it on his face…

She was so embarrassed and scared and disappointed that she couldn't look at him anymore. She closed her eyes.

"Sharon—"

But whatever he had been about to say to her was lost as the shooting began….

The shooting outside the estate distracted the judge enough that Parker managed to step between Sharon and the gun pointed at her.

Parker flinched, waiting for the gun to go off. But the judge just continued to hold the weapon. Maybe he was more used to others doing his dirty work than doing it himself.

"What the hell's going on?" he asked. But he wasn't even looking at Parker; he obviously didn't expect him to know.

But Parker knew that the gunfire throughout the estate was Payne Protection Agency coming to his and Sharon's rescue just as he and Logan had planned. They must have overpowered Munson's motley mix of dirty cops and convicts by now.

The judge glanced toward the door and gasped. Parker followed his gaze and gasped, too. The man standing in the doorway with a gun wasn't a Payne—at least not a legitimate one—although he looked exactly like one.

"Agent Rus," Parker murmured. "What the hell are you doing here?"

The judge tightened his grasp on the gun, obviously uncertain whose side the federal agent was on; he wasn't the only one.

The agent grinned, an expression of which Parker wouldn't have thought him capable. "I'm here to collect the reward," he said.

And Parker's guts tightened with dread. "What?"

"They're both still alive," the judge pointed out.

The agent held up a small piece of plastic. "The flash drive. I suspect this might be worth more than the two of them combined."

"What do you know?" the judge asked.

"A few days before Payne here killed him, Detective Sharpe told me everything," the agent replied. He snorted derisively. "Not sure how such an idiot made detective in the first place."

The judge's eyes widened in surprise. "Sharpe talked?"

"You didn't think he would?"

"Given the amount of money I was paying him, I thought he would keep his damn mouth shut." The judge sighed. "I should have known better than to trust him. I should know better than to trust anyone."

And it was obvious he didn't trust Agent Rus yet.

"Where did you get that?" the judge asked with a suspicious glance at the flash drive. He probably thought it was as empty as the one Parker had brought him.

Parker was afraid that it wasn't. And his guts twisted with fear over how the agent might have come to possess it.

"Mrs. Payne walked into the police department and handed it right to me," Rus replied. "She found it in her grandson's diaper bag."

That was why his mother had come down to the police

department—not to bail him out, but because she had found what everyone had been looking for. Of course, she probably hadn't known it was what everyone was looking for—just that it was suspicious to find in a diaper bag. Or, knowing his mother's curiosity, she may have opened and read the files on it.

"Did you hurt her?" he asked. He didn't care that the bastard was armed; if he'd hurt his mother any more than his mere existence already had, Parker would take him out with his bare hands like the bodyguard had Brenda.

Rus shook his head.

"Did she see what was on it?" the judge asked.

Rus shook his head again. "She has no idea what's on it." His grin flashed again, making him look even more like Cooper. But he was nothing like Parker's marine brother, who had put his life on the line for years for his country. "But *I* looked at it," he said. "I know what's on it."

Parker had always thought the dirtiest cops were the ones who investigated other cops—like Rus was doing for the feds. At least he hadn't been wrong about that.

His eyes narrowed with suspicion, the judge asked, "What was all the shooting we just heard? What happened out there?"

The fed uttered a condescending chuckle. "You didn't think Parker Payne would really come here alone, did you?"

It obviously hadn't occurred to the judge that Parker hadn't walked alone into his trap. He wasn't the idiot that Sharpe had been. Regrettably, neither was Nicholas Rus.

"That family travels in a pack—" Rus snorted "—like wild dogs."

Parker silently cursed the loss of his weapon because he wanted to use it on Rus. Badly.

"His brothers are out there?" Munson asked.

He nodded. "They were. Even the little sister was—she must have trailed after them."

Nikki had tagged along to the estate even though Parker hadn't wanted her along. And neither had Logan. But she had insisted on helping, and he hadn't wanted to waste time arguing with her. Now he wished that he had….

Horror and fear struck Parker's heart, and Sharon gasped, choking on a sob. She hadn't known them long, but she had obviously already come to love his family like her own. They had been hers—for a little while.

They had been his all his life. His mother had already lost his father; she couldn't lose all of her children, too. Maybe Rus was wrong; maybe his family had survived. Parker had to get to them, had to figure out how to help them.

The judge was concerned, too—about himself. "How are we going to clean up the mess?" he asked Rus.

"What about the guy you hired to place all those bombs?" Rus asked. "Can't he set up another little explosion?"

"There were actually a couple of guys that set those bombs," the judge replied. "But he—" he gestured toward Parker "—killed them in the street."

Rus shrugged. "I have a military background. I was deployed in Afghanistan." Like Cooper had been, but Cooper was a hero. Rus was a killer. "I'll set the bomb."

"Not here," the judge vehemently replied.

"You have to," Rus insisted. "You'll never clean it up enough that a crime tech couldn't find blood or DNA."

Sharon gasped again, as if she couldn't breathe. She wept for his family.

Parker felt sick. He wouldn't have involved his family if he hadn't believed that they would all survive. This was his fault—all his fault.

The judge's voice cracked, as if he was close to tears, too, as he said, "I've worked too hard for my estate—everything I've done I've done to keep this place."

"It's just a house," Rus said dismissively. If he didn't care about possessions, why had he killed for money?

"It wasn't just about the house," the judge said. "It was about the money and prestige, which I needed to keep my wife."

Rus glanced around as if looking for Mrs. Munson. "Is she here?"

He wasn't going to find her.

Parker pushed aside his pain to focus on their conversation, to force himself to find a way out for him and Sharon.

The judge shook his head. "In the end, the money wasn't enough for her."

Parker opened his mouth to correct the fed's misconception about Mrs. Munson. He had recalled what had become of her. But a gesture from Rus stopped him.

The man shook his head, as if commiserating with the judge. "So you took all those bribes and she still left you?"

The judge nodded. "I took dirty money—money from criminals to either throw out the cases against them or reduce their sentences."

"But your wife didn't leave you," Parker said, unable to hold his tongue any longer. "She was killed."

The judge laughed. "Do you think I would let her

divorce me after everything I'd done for her? She wasn't going to take anything else from me."

"So you had one of those criminals kill her?" Parker asked the question now. He wanted to know how long this man had been a killer.

"Hell, I did that myself," the judge said. "Right here in this solarium and had that dim-witted Sharpe kid help me clean up the scene. Too bad he's dead."

"I'll do your dirty work," Rus said. "But I want more than that reward you offered."

Parker had no choice. He had to act now or he'd miss his opportunity. It didn't matter if he got shot as long as he gave Sharon the opportunity to escape. He knocked her chair to the ground, hoping that the wicker might break or crack and loosen the ropes that he had been unable to undo.

And then he vaulted himself at Rus; he had to overpower him or die trying. But something struck his jaw, and darkness filled his vision. He fought to remain conscious so that he could protect Sharon, so that he could tell her that he loved her....

Chapter Nineteen

As Parker's eyes rolled back in his head, Sharon screamed. Was he dead? She struggled against the ropes and finally they were loose enough that she slipped her wrists free of the bindings. Then she crawled over to Parker's side and cradled his head on her lap. At least she had told him that she loved him....

His pulse flickered beneath the skin of his throat. He wasn't dead. Yet. But she doubted it would be much longer before this man—this man who looked so much like Parker—killed them both.

The judge stared at Parker on the floor. "So what do you want?" he asked Rus. "What do you want as your reward for killing these two and cleaning up the mess? How much is this going to cost me?"

Sharon shuddered as the federal agent grinned. How could he have killed a whole family and been so smug about it? If he was that heartless, there was no way that he was really a Payne.

But then the man replied, "You can keep your money, Judge. My reward will be you behind bars, Your Honor—for the rest of your life."

She had forgotten the judge still held his gun—until

he fired it—right into the federal agent's chest. The man dropped to the ground next to her and Parker.

The judge shook his head with self-disgust. "Should have known I couldn't trust a Payne. Even a bastard one has more integrity than intelligence."

Then he turned the weapon on Parker and Sharon. But Parker was no longer unconscious on her lap—he was leaping up and vaulting toward the judge. The gun went off again, the shots echoing throughout the room, shattering the glass walls.

Parker flinched. But he didn't feel the unmistakable burn of being struck by a bullet. Or maybe he was too numb with pain over the loss of his family to feel it. But were they really lost?

Footsteps pounded against the slate tiles of the solarium floor. He glanced over his shoulder to see Logan and Cooper rushing into the room. If they'd been hurt, they wouldn't have been able to move with such speed.

"You guys aren't dead," Parker remarked with a sigh of relief.

Logan shook his head. "No..."

But, remembering all the shooting, Parker bet some other lives had been lost. "Where were you, then?"

"We had to revise the plan," Logan said.

The judge squirmed beneath him, fighting him for the gun. Parker smacked the older man's wrist against the ground until the Glock skidded across the tile floor. Cooper grabbed the weapon.

Without his gun and his authority, the judge was just a pathetic old man. And as he realized and accepted that, his shoulders began to shake with sobs. Parker rolled off him and turned back toward Sharon.

She was sitting up and appeared to be unharmed. But

she wouldn't look at Parker; her attention was focused on the one person who had been hurt in the room.

Parker knelt beside the prone body of the man who looked so much like him and his brothers. The federal agent's eyes were closed.

Rus had saved his life. But what had it cost him? His own?

Parker asked, "Can you hear me?"

"Yes." The federal agent coughed and groaned and sat up. "Yes, but only thanks to this bulletproof vest, courtesy of River City P.D. I knew I never should have come here."

Parker would have agreed a short while ago, but the man had saved his and his family's lives. Maybe Rus wasn't the outsider Parker had thought him; maybe he could one day think of this man as his brother.

Rus fumbled with the buttons on his shirt. Then Velcro ripped as he opened the side of his vest and reached beneath it. Had he been hit? He grunted and squirmed and remarked, "Hope the impact of the bullet didn't short out a wire."

"You were wired?" the judge asked as Logan and Cooper helped him to his feet. He was an old man but, aware of how dangerous he was, they both held on to him.

"Yeah, I got it all on tape," Rus told the judge.

"That was the reason you revised the plan," Parker realized. But he was surprised Logan had taken orders from anyone, let alone Rus.

Logan shrugged. "Without the wire, it would have just been his word against yours and Sharon's."

And Munson was a respected judge. Or he had been....

Parker turned back to Rus. "Did you have to make me think my family was dead?" He had never been so devastated in his life.

"I had to make him trust me enough to talk," Rus pointed out. "And explain all the shooting...."

Parker sighed and nodded acceptance.

"And I got everything we need," Rus reminded him as he patted his vest.

Parker turned back to the murderous judge. "There will be no case thrown out or reduced sentences for you."

It was over. It was finally over.

Parker heaved a sigh of relief and turned toward Sharon. But only the broken wicker chair lay on the floor where she had been sitting; she was gone.

"What happened to my wife?" he asked. While he had been checking on Rus to make sure he wasn't dead, she must have slipped away.

"She met Nikki in the doorway," Cooper replied. "And they took off."

Had they told Nikki to stay outside the room until the judge was disarmed? Or hadn't she wanted to come any closer to Nicholas Rus?

She must have been devastated to meet their half *brother.* No one had idolized their father more than she had. That explained why Nikki had left so abruptly.

Why had Sharon? Was she hurt? Or in shock again after everything she'd endured?

Where had his bride gone?

SHARON'S ARMS TREMBLED as she clutched the baby close to her heart. Ethan had already claimed it for his own. She hadn't realized she had had more love left to give until she had fallen for Parker, too. But then, for so many years, she'd had no one who had wanted to accept or give her love.

Neither did Parker, though.

He had been so horrified when she'd confessed her feelings for him. Her face heated with embarrassment as she remembered the look on his face, the regret. To save them both from further embarrassment, she had to leave before he came to see his son, too.

But her arms refused to budge from around the baby. She had gone so long without holding Ethan that she couldn't release him. His warm little squirmy body gave her comfort. He was all right....

His breath hitched and then raggedly shuddered out with relief.

"He missed you so much," Mrs. Payne remarked as she reached out. Sharon thought she'd been reaching for her grandson, but instead her palm skimmed across Sharon's cheek. "Are you all right, honey?"

"It's all over now." Thanks to Parker. And to the man who looked so much like a Payne. Who was he?

"I knocked over the diaper bag earlier today and the flash drive fell out," Mrs. Payne shared. "I didn't want to pry into your life, so I didn't look at it. But I wanted to get it to you in case it was important."

It was far more important than she had realized.

"So you gave it to *him?*" Nikki asked. "You trusted something that important to *him?*" She had driven Sharon to Mrs. Payne's, but she hadn't said much in the car. And she hadn't said a word since arriving at her mother's. Hollow-eyed and pale, she looked as devastated as Sharon felt.

"I was going to give it to Sharon," Mrs. Payne reminded her, "but she had already left the police department."

Because the judge had bailed her out. She shuddered

even now, remembering how easily he had led her out of the police station at gunpoint.

If not for Parker and his family, she would have been dead. She never would have been able to hold Ethan again. But she wasn't sure that she would be able to again….

"And when Parker realized she was in danger," Mrs. Payne continued, "he was too upset to listen to me."

"Or were *you* too upset?" Nikki asked. "Wasn't it a shock to see *him?*" She had obviously been shocked to learn she had another brother and she was still in shock.

Mrs. Payne sighed. "This is neither the time nor the place to discuss this…."

Because Sharon wasn't family.

When Parker had put that ring on her finger, she had fooled herself into thinking their marriage was real, that his wonderful family might become hers. But now she was more alone than she had ever been. She had no one anymore.

"Sharon's a Payne, too," Nikki said, inclusively. "She deserves to know what's going on, too."

Sharon shook her head. "It's fine. Really," she assured Nikki. "I—I just wanted to see Ethan."

She had no right to their secrets—not unless she had Parker's love. And she didn't. If he'd had any feelings for her, he would have reciprocated her declaration of love—especially then, when they had been about to die.

"Thank you for bringing me here," she told Nikki.

Mrs. Payne's soft yellow farmhouse with a wraparound porch was as warm and inviting as her little white wedding chapel. She could imagine Parker and his brothers and sister growing up here. She could imagine Parker sneaking kisses on that porch swing with whatever girl he had been dating that day….

She doubted his relationships had ever lasted much longer than that. Their marriage had barely lasted a day. But the night…

Her skin warmed at just the memory of the heat of his kisses, his passion….

She had been a fool to think that she—awkward, inexperienced Sharon Wells—had ever had a chance with a playboy like Parker Payne.

Nikki nodded. "I didn't want to stick around there and watch *him* play hero anymore. We didn't need him interfering. We'd had it all under control…."

Mrs. Payne turned her attention to her daughter. "Honey, don't be angry with him. It's not his fault…."

Tears glistened in Nikki's eyes. "No, it was Dad's…."

Mrs. Payne reached for her, but Nikki whirled around and ran out of the living room. She didn't stop on the front porch but kept running to where she had left her car parked in the gravel driveway.

"Will she be okay?" Sharon asked.

Mrs. Payne nodded. "Of course. She's stronger than she knows—certainly stronger than her brothers realize."

"Does she have another brother? Is Nicholas Rus her half brother?" Sharon asked then flushed with embarrassment at her nosiness. "Forget I asked—"

"He is a Payne," the older woman admitted with a heavy sigh. Suddenly lines appeared on her beautiful face, and she actually looked her age. "My husband used to be an undercover cop just like Parker had been when he'd been with the River City Police Department. Nick—my husband—got really caught up in an assignment and with a witness who had been in danger…."

Was that what had happened with her and Parker on their wedding night? Had he just gotten caught up in the moment, in the danger? Was that why he'd made love to her?

Tears sparkled in Mrs. Payne's warm brown eyes. "He didn't know that she was pregnant...."

"I'm sorry," Sharon said. Her heart ached for the woman's pain even as her own heart filled with it.

Mrs. Payne blinked back her tears, obviously embarrassed. "It's fine...."

"I shouldn't have asked," Sharon said with her own embarrassment. "It's none of my business."

Mrs. Payne wrapped her arm around Sharon's shoulders. "Of course it is. You are family now."

Sharon shook her head. "No. My marriage to Parker was never real."

"You have a marriage license that proves it is," Mrs. Payne insisted.

"Considering who issued it, I'm not sure that's true anymore," Sharon reminded her. "But that's okay. It was never meant to last—only to protect Ethan." She forced herself to pass the little boy into his grandmother's arms, but he clutched at her hair, tangling it around his pudgy fingers. She teared up, but not over the pain of him tugging at her scalp. But over what she had to do, which was walk away.

"He's safe now...."

"It's really all over now?" Mrs. Payne asked.

Sharon nodded. It was all over. Her marriage. Her involvement in the Paynes' lives. It didn't matter that Brenda had appointed her Ethan's guardian; she wasn't his family. He had an amazing family that would care for him no matter what. Today had proved that to her—how they had all been there for each other, including the man they hadn't even known was a brother.

The Paynes took care of their own; they would take care of Ethan.

Sharon drew in a deep breath, bracing herself, before she replied, "Yes, it's all over now. And it's time for me to leave."

Chapter Twenty

Parker had a tight knot of fear and dread in his gut and he didn't know why. It was all over. Even the judge had known it was over and had confessed everything, as if that might make amends for all the evil he had done, for all the innocent lives that had been lost because of him.

Parker pushed open the door to the house where he had grown up, and that knot eased slightly when the little boy in his mother's arms smiled at him as if he knew him, as if he was beginning to love him as much as Parker already loved him.

Parker stepped closer, and the little boy reached out for him. Long strands of caramel-colored hair dangled from his pudgy fingers. And that knot eased even more. "Sharon's here?"

He took the little boy from his mother, welcoming his slight weight and his warmth. Ethan smelled like sunshine and rain, like Sharon.

His mother shook her head. "She's gone…."

She said it with a finality that had that knot tightening in his gut again.

"Where? How?" She had no car, no place left to go. "Did Nikki take her somewhere?" he asked since his sister's car wasn't parked in the driveway.

Mom sighed. "No. Nikki left first…."

He heard the distress in his mother's voice, and cradling his son with one arm, he slid his other one around her shoulders. "She's not upset with you."

"I'm not so sure about that," she replied, her voice cracking with emotion.

"It's not your fault…." That their father had an illegitimate son. "It was his."

"Is it your fault that Sharon left?" she asked him. "Because I can't believe that she would leave…."

"She's really gone?" he asked. That knot tightened so much that he couldn't draw a deep breath. He shook his head. "She wouldn't leave Ethan."

She loved that little boy so much. She had also said that she loved *him.* But he hadn't said the words back to her. It was his fault.

"She thinks he doesn't need her because he has us," Mrs. Payne replied. She shook her head as if she found the idea as ridiculous as he did.

"That's crazy," Parker replied. "He loves her like she's his mother."

As if in agreement, the little boy shook his fist full of those strands of hair. Parker could not blame his son for wanting to hang on to her. Sharon Wells Payne was an amazing woman—a strong, loving woman.

"Do you love her?" Mrs. Payne asked.

Parker shook his head.

"You don't?" she asked, her voice full of shock as her eyes widened.

"It doesn't matter what I feel for her," he explained. "She'll be better off without me."

"Why would you say that?" she asked. "The danger is past, right? The judge has been arrested?"

"Yes." Thanks to Nicholas Rus. "He'll go away for the rest of his life, at least." He would be serving time with criminals. But the only ones of them that he had put behind bars would have been the ones unable to afford his bribes. Parker couldn't imagine they would be very happy or forgiving.

His mother's usually smooth brow furrowed with confusion. "Then why in the world would you think she would be better off without you?"

"Do you know why I never intended to get married and have kids?" he asked her.

She nodded. "Because of how we lost your father..." She gently touched his cheek. "You always acted the silliest of all the kids, but I think that's because the loss of your father affected you the most."

"It affected *you* the most," he said. "And I didn't want to do that to my wife. I didn't want to leave someone behind to mourn me like you did Dad." And now, knowing what he did, he was surprised that she had. He was surprised that she had been able to forgive him at all.

"That's crazy," his mother said, dismissing his fears as easily as she had when he'd been a kid afraid of the boogeyman in his closet.

"You don't know that anything will happen to you," she said. "You could live to be an old man."

Like his father should have....

He shrugged. "No, but the protection business is about protecting other people, not ourselves."

"The past two weeks you have been in more danger than you ever were on the police force or as a bodyguard," she pointed out with a shiver of residual fear. "You had a price on your head."

"A big price," he admitted with a shiver of his own.

Garek and Milek had promised to get out the word that there was no way anyone could collect that reward with the judge in jail for the rest of his life.

"And you survived these past few weeks," she pointed out. "You're a survivor. We all are…."

He nodded in agreement. She was right. Cooper had survived a few deployments to war-torn countries. Logan and he had both survived numerous attempts on their lives.

"But dying is not the only way I might hurt my wife," he said.

Her hand stilled on his cheek. "What do you mean?"

"Of all of us kids, I'm the most like Dad." He reminded her of what she had always told him. Now he finally understood why she had thought that. "I'm a playboy. I'm not husband or father material."

But his arm tightened around his son. He *wanted* to be, for Ethan and for Sharon.

"Sharon will be better off without me." Because she had fallen for him, just as he had feared she would, he could hurt her so badly…like his father must have hurt his mother.

Her hand moved again and softly struck his cheek. "You're an idiot."

"Just another way I'm like Dad," he bitterly remarked. "I can't believe he cheated on you." And that she must have forgiven and taken him back since Nikki was younger than the federal agent.

Her breath shuddered out in a shaky sigh. "He regretted that so much. It happened when he was undercover. He had gotten so caught up in the assignment. And he was in so much danger. He and Carla both were. If he hadn't acted his part completely…"

Parker nodded in sudden understanding. "He could have given himself away."

"He told me right away." She shuddered. "I was already pregnant with Cooper. And I loved him so much...."

"So you forgave him?"

"On one condition," she said. Her voice cracked as if that condition had cost her.

He lifted a brow and waited.

"That he would never go undercover again," she said. "He went back to being a uniformed officer. And that's what killed him. My one condition..."

"Mom..."

"If he hadn't been in uniform, he wouldn't have had a partner—the partner who betrayed him." Tears streamed down her face. "It's all my fault."

He tightened his arm around her. She must have spent the past fifteen years blaming herself for her husband's death. No wonder she had mourned him so much. "Mom, it's not your fault. None of what happened was your fault. Not his cheating and not his death."

She leaned against his side, and her tears wetted his shirt. "When I told you that you were the most like your father," she said, "I meant that you are protective and loving. I forgave him for what happened, but he never forgave himself. He spent the rest of his life making it up to me and loving me. He was the best husband and father, and you will be, too, Parker."

"But what if I...?" He couldn't even say it; he would never even consider cheating on Sharon. He loved her too much to ever want another woman.

His mother must have seen it dawn on him because she smiled. "Go find your bride," she urged him.

But he didn't know where to look for her. She had no

car. No house. No job. She had nothing to keep her in River City…but him and their son.

He passed Ethan back to his grandmother and kissed the boy's forehead. "I'm going to go find your mama," he said. "And bring her home, where she belongs."

With their family…

SHARON HAD SPENT most of her life alone, so she didn't know why it felt so strange to her now. She didn't know why her new apartment was so quiet and empty….

She had once appreciated silence in order to study. But she didn't care to study now. She had no intention of trying to pass the bar again. She had only studied law in order to please her grandfather, but she should have known there would have been no pleasing him—even when he'd been alive. There was definitely no pleasing him now.

But she couldn't please herself, either…or she would be back with Ethan. She would be holding her little man. But she would also be begging Parker for his love. And she had begged for love for too much of her life. She wanted it given freely to her.

She dropped one of the pillows she had bought onto the couch and stepped back. The orange looked good against the chocolate suede. Maybe she could become a decorator.

But it didn't matter what she did to the apartment; it would never be a home like Mrs. Payne had made for her family. But Sharon didn't have a family….

She glanced down at the ring on her finger, the ring Parker Payne had slid there when they had said their vows. She needed to take off the gold band. It wasn't as if their marriage was real….

That was why she hadn't contacted a lawyer yet to start divorce proceedings. She doubted anything Judge Munson had signed would prove legal. Of course, it had been only a couple of days since she had kissed Ethan goodbye. A couple of days that she had filled with finding an apartment and buying a car and clothes. She'd intended to stay so busy that she didn't miss the little boy or his father.

But it hadn't worked. They were both forever on her mind. She grabbed the pillow and wrapped her arms around it. But it wasn't warm and squirmy like her little man. Or hard and hot like her big man…

They weren't hers, though. They had never really been hers.

Tears stung her eyes, but she blinked them back. Then she breathed a sigh of relief when the doorbell rang. Whatever delivery had come was certain to distract her from her self-pity. But when she opened the door, the reason for all of her pain stood on her doorstep.

He looked so handsome—even with dark circles beneath his blue eyes and his black hair tousled as if he'd been running his hands through it. He also looked angry. And his words confirmed it. "I am so damn mad at you."

"Why?" she asked, stepping back as he pushed his way inside her apartment.

He slammed the door behind himself and followed her, backing her up until she ran into the new sofa. "I thought you loved Ethan."

Tears stung her eyes again. "I do. Of course I do. Is he all right?"

"No," he said.

And panic struck her heart. She had thought the little

boy would be safe and happy with his family. "What's wrong? What's happened to him?"

"He misses you," Parker said.

She closed her eyes to hold in her tears. She missed him, too—so very much. "He's so young," she pointed out. "He'll soon forget all about me."

"What about me?" he asked with such forlornness that she opened her eyes and stared up into his face.

He was so handsome that it wasn't fair. How could she have not fallen in love with him? She wasn't as weak as everyone always thought her, but she wasn't strong enough to resist a man like him.

"What about you?" she asked, unable to understand his question.

"I miss you, too," he said.

"You'll forget me, too," she assured him. She was actually surprised that he hadn't already. That he hadn't already moved on to the next woman—one far more beautiful and carefree than his bride.

He shook his head. "I've been going crazy trying to find you. I was worried that you had left town, maybe even the state."

"Agent Rus told me that I might need to testify at the judge's sentencing hearing." She had gone down to the department to give her statement. Seeing the agent looking so much like Parker had been hard. But she'd wanted to do the right thing. Had the agent? "Did Rus tell you where to find me?"

Parker cracked his knuckles. "With a little coercion..."

"You didn't fight with him, did you?" Not over her. They needed to build a relationship, not destroy the tenuous bond they'd formed over the judge's arrest.

He sighed. "That pain in the neck loved it, loved to see me beg."

"You begged?" she asked. And now she was totally confused. First by his anger and now by the look in his eyes. They were so intense, so focused on her.

"Are you going to make me beg, too?"

"For what?" If he wanted her, she was powerless to resist him. Since she had opened the door to find him on her doorstep, her pulse had been racing. And her skin was hot and tingling just from the touch of his gaze....

His eyes were such a bright blue—like his son's. She had always been a sucker for those eyes.

"For you," he said. "For another chance..."

"Another chance?" She hadn't realized they had ever had one.

He stepped closer to her, so that his body brushed against hers. "Tell me you love me again."

Now her skin heated with the flush of embarrassment, and she shook her head.

"So you only told me that because you thought you were going to die?" he asked, his voice gruff with disappointment. "Not because you really have any feelings for me?"

"What does it matter now?" she asked. He didn't return her feelings.

"I thought you were only saying them because you thought you were going to die," he said. "And I was sorry that I couldn't let you know that I hadn't come alone, that Logan and Cooper were waiting for their chance to come to our rescue."

She didn't know what to say. Should she admit that fear had had nothing to do with her admission? That she really loved him? But if he had come to her only out of pity…

He continued, "But then Logan and Cooper didn't come in…." And he shuddered as he must have recalled those horrible moments they'd believed they were dead.

"Your other brother came to the rescue," she reminded him.

He flinched as she said it, so she lifted her hand and touched his chest, her palm over his heart. It pounded hard and fast as if he was in danger.

"I'm sorry," she said. "Sorry that you didn't know about him."

He shrugged. "Nicholas Rus is a Payne—whether he wants to be one or not."

So there were other issues with the federal agent. But Parker shrugged and focused on her again with that intense gaze.

"What about you?" he asked. "Do you want to be a Payne?"

Her breath caught, but she refused to let herself hope. "What are you asking me?"

"You haven't started divorce proceedings," he said.

She shrugged now. "Do I need to? The marriage isn't real."

"Yes, it is," he said. "Because he was a judge at the time he signed it, the license is valid. What about the marriage?"

"We're safe now," she reminded him. But she hadn't felt safe even though the federal agent had assured her that everyone knew they could no longer collect any reward for her murder. She had only felt safe in Parker's arms. "For our safety and for Ethan's were the only reasons we got married."

"And you're going to let me just have Ethan?" he asked. "You're not going to fight me for him?"

"You're his father," she said. "I'm nothing but his previous nanny."

The anger was back, darkening his blue eyes. "You're everything to that little boy." He touched her now, cupping her face in both his hands. "And you're everything to me, Sharon. I love you, and I want to spend the rest of my life with you."

She froze, unable to comprehend what he was telling her. Nobody but her mother had ever said those words to her, and that had been so long ago that she'd forgotten how they'd sounded, and how it felt to hear them. "You what?"

"I love you," he said. And as if he knew she couldn't understand his words, he proved his love with actions. He kissed her—gently at first and then with all the passion that he had on their wedding night. And then he laid her down on the couch and made love to her body.

In the frenzy of movement, she didn't even notice when he took off her clothes; she realized only that she was naked beneath him. And he was kissing her…intimately… while his fingers teased her peaked nipples. She squirmed as pressure mounted inside her; her skin tingled and heated from his touch. She wanted him so much—wanted the pleasure she knew he could give her. Then he sucked on her most sensitive place, and that pleasure came, overwhelming her so that she screamed his name.

And he filled her, thrusting inside her—joining their bodies. He wasn't as gentle as he had been on their wedding night, when he'd been worried that she was hurt from the collision. He made love to her now like a man overcome with desire.

She clutched him with her arms and her legs, matching his thrusts until she climaxed again—with him. And as he filled her with his pleasure, he kept declaring his love again and again.

Panting for breath, she sank deeper into the cushions of the couch, and he gently pushed her damp hair from her face. Then he stared into her eyes again, as if trying to let her see inside him—into his heart and soul.

"I will keep professing my love until you believe me," he promised.

"Don't stop even then," she said, as tears stung her eyes and began to run down her face. "Don't ever stop telling me."

Because she hadn't heard those words in so long....

He must have realized when she had heard them last because he kissed her damp eyes and murmured, "I'm sorry, sweetheart. So sorry you didn't get the love you deserved all these years. But I will spend the rest of my life making it up to you. You have my love and Ethan's. And our entire family loves you, too."

She was so overwhelmed with happiness that she just clung to him and cried happy tears. And finally when she could catch her breath again, she told him, "I love you. I love you so much."

"Then you will stay married to me?" he asked hopefully. "You will be my wife and Ethan's mother and Penny's daughter and Logan and Cooper and Nikki's sister?"

"You are giving me so much," she said. Everything she had always wanted. A family. "I have nothing to give to you...." Except for money, but she knew him well enough to know that money didn't matter to Parker Payne.

He shook his head. "Sweetheart, you have given me

everything. You are *everything* to me. You are my life. And I want to spend the rest of it with you."

She wrapped her arms around his neck and pulled him down for her kiss. "I love you."

She had probably always known that she would fall for her playboy protector, but she hadn't realized that he would fall for her, too.

But then he was telling her again—just as he had promised—over and over. "I love you."

She looked forward to hearing those words for the rest of their lives together.

* * * * *

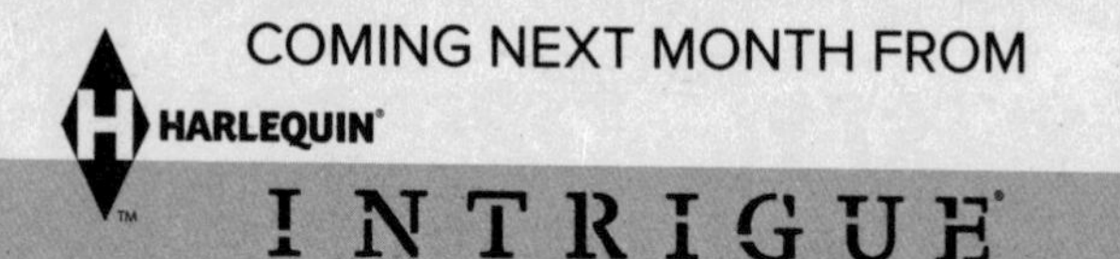

Available August 19, 2014

#1515 MAVERICK SHERIFF
Sweetwater Ranch • by Delores Fossen

Thrown into a dangerous investigation, Sheriff Cooper McKinnon and Assistant District Attorney Jessa Wells must join forces to protect the baby they each claim as their own.

#1516 WAY OF THE SHADOWS
Shadow Agents: Guts and Glory • by Cynthia Eden

FBI profiler Noelle Evers can't remember him...but former army ranger Thomas Anthony would kill in order to protect the one woman he can't live without. With Noelle once again in a predator's sights, can Thomas save the woman he loves a second time?

#1517 DEAD MAN'S CURVE
The Gates • by Paula Graves

When CIA double agent Sinclair Solano is lured out of hiding to recover his kidnapped sister, he crosses swords with a beautiful FBI agent, Ava Trent, who wants him—dead or alive.

#1518 THE WHARF
Brody Law • by Carol Ericson

Police Chief Ryan Brody trusts true-crime writer Kacie Manning to help him catch a killer, but Kacie is keeping a dark secret from him. Can Kacie abandon her quest for revenge to give their love a chance...or will the *real* psychopath get to her first?

#1519 SNOW BLIND
by Cassie Miles

After witnessing a murder, Sasha Campbell turns to local sheriff's deputy Brady Ellis for protection. But while Brady and Sasha grow closer to one another, the killer gets dangerously closer to them.

#1520 STALKED
The Men from Crow Hollow • by Beverly Long

Tabloid celebrity Hope Minnow believes recent death threats are a publicity stunt and refuses navy intelligence officer turned bodyguard Mack McCann's protection. But when the threats turn very real, can Mack get to Hope in time to save her?

Thrown into a dangerous investigation, Sheriff Cooper McKinnon and Assistant District Attorney Jessa Wells must join forces to protect the baby they each claim as their own.

Read on for an excerpt from MAVERICK SHERIFF
The first installment in the **SWEETWATER RANCH** *series*
by USA TODAY *bestselling author* Delores Fossen

"You had my son's DNA tested, why?" Jessa demanded. But that was as far as she got. Her chest started pumping as if starved for air, and she dropped back and let the now closed door support her.

The dark circles under her eyes let him know she hadn't been sleeping.

Neither had he.

It'd taken every ounce of willpower for him not to rush back to the hospital to get a better look at the little boy.

"How's Liam?" he asked.

She glared at him for so long that Cooper wasn't sure she'd answer. "He's better, but you already know that. You've called at least a dozen times checking on his condition."

He had. Cooper also knew Liam was doing so well that he'd probably be released from the hospital tomorrow.

"He'll make a full recovery?" Cooper asked.

Again, she glared. "Yes. In fact, he already wants to get up and run around. Now, why?" she added without pausing.

Cooper pulled in a long breath that he would need and sank down on the edge of his desk. "Because of the blood type match. And because we never found my son's body."

Even though she'd no doubt already come up with that

HIEXP69782

answer, Jessa huffed and threw her hands in the air. "And what? You think I found him on the riverbank and pretended to adopt him? Well, I didn't, and Liam's not your son. I want you to put a stop to that DNA test."

Cooper shook his head. "If you're sure he's not my son, then the test will come back as no match."

Her glare got worse. "You're doing this to get back at me." Her breath broke, and the tears came.

Oh, man.

He didn't want this. Not with both of them already emotional wrecks. They were both powder kegs right now, and the flames were shooting all around them. Still, he went closer, and because all those emotions had apparently made him dumber than dirt, Cooper slipped his arm around her.

She fought him. Of course. Jessa clearly didn't want his comfort, sympathy or anything else other than an assurance to put a stop to that test. Still, he held on despite her fists pushing against his chest. One more ragged sob, however, and she sagged against him.

There it was again. That tug deep down in his body. Yeah, dumber than dirt, all right. His body just didn't seem to understand that an attractive woman in his arms could mean nothing.

Even when Jessa looked up at him.

That tug tugged a little harder. Because, yeah, she was attractive, and if the investigation and accusations hadn't cropped up, he might have considered asking her out.

So much for that plan.